I0666393

Strip Him!

First Edition

Will Scott

Strip Him!

First Edition

Published by
The Nazca Plains Corporation
Las Vegas, Nevada
2007

ISBN: 978-1-887895-96-5

Published by

The Nazca Plains Corporation ®
4640 Paradise Rd, Suite 141
Las Vegas NV 89109-8000

PUBLISHER'S NOTE
Strip Him! is a work of fiction created wholly by *Will Scott's* imagi-
nation. All characters are fictional and any resemblance to any
persons living or deceased is purely by accident. No portion of
this book reflects any real person or events.

Cover Art, Greasetank
Art Director, Blake Stephens

Strip Him!

Will Scott

Contents

Dieter *Rache*

"Rache" Revenge, Dieter screamed as he watched the life-less and mangled body of his older brother Heinrich carried by the Wien Polizei from the car. Through his bitter tears of rage he spotted the driver of the truck that had rammed into his brother's car.

A young Turk, Egon was his name, sat on the curb holding his bruised head in his hands while steam shot forth from the hood of his smashed pickup truck. Dieter made a frantic lurch for Egon but the quick thinking police managed to hold him back.

"I'll kill you." Dieter shouted as he struggled like a man pos-sessed.

"Calm, calm down, let the medics take a look at you," cau-tioned one of the attending cops.

"Nien, Nien, let me go, let me fuckin' go" Dieter demanded. The arrival of the paramedics attending Egon made any further protestations useless. He must find out where this bastard lived, get his comrades together. Make the fucker pay. Only thing left to do now was follow his brother's lifeless body into the ambu-lance. The only person that Dieter loved was his older brother Whilhelm. The two brothers shared more than a passion for a body building; when they were together they fed on each other's violent souls, cruising the back alleys of working class Vienna, hunting for the weak and foreign. They found release from their own rage and self loathing by stomping and robbing young immigrant men. Their wild brawls became sexual encounters between the two brothers. Like two halves when joined together they turned into a single monstrous evil. And now that one half of the duo was gone Dieter felt lost and alone beyond any pain he had ever experienced.

Egon through the fog of pain and shock tried to remember what happened. He was driving down the Ringstrasses near the Kunsthistorische Museum when the silver BMW traveling like a race car went through the light and BAM he plowed into the driver's side of another car. It was like a bolt of lightning from the sky, suddenly out of nowhere screeching brakes, broken glasses and blood were everywhere. The passenger from the BMW climbed out and started screaming at him just before the cops came. It wasn't his fault but he knew how it would look, a Turk, who just moved to Vienna, and was poor, against two rich blond Austrians. He didn't stand a chance. He should try to call his lover Cri at the coffee shop. That was his last thought for awhile as he felt dizzy and passed out into the waiting arms of the ambulance attendants.

Cri leaned over the hospital bed and said, "Egon, Egon can you hear me?"

"Let him rest" the nurse snapped as she went about adjusting his IV. "He has a bad head injury" she added with a touch of compassion. Seeing the look on Cri's face she added, "You shouldn't worry, he will be fine in a day or two then you can take him home then. Are you his brother?"

"No, we are friends."

"I understand" said the nurse knowingly. They must have it tough, gay and Turk; a double handicap, strangers in a strange land and outsiders to their own people, sad she thought.

"Thank you. Is it alright if I sit here with him?"

"Yes certainly. You can stay until nine, then you must leave. Don't worry so much."

"I won't, thank you again."

The nurse finished up her chores and left as Cri settled in a stiff backed plastic chair.

How handsome, he thought of Egon his lover. His thick luxurious raven hair, his perfect olive complexion; always with a few days growth of black stubble that made him appear all the more masculine, and those deep green eyes; some left over from an ancient Byzantine ancestor. Cri remembered the first time he saw Egon. It was in a Banyosu, steam bath in Ankara. Through the clouds of mist he spotted his future friend and lover laying on a marble bench with a towel folded as a pillow for his head. His naked body glistened like a Greek sculpture, the gentle rise and fall of his magnificent chest; lightly dusted with curling black hair that lapped provocatively around each of his perfectly formed nipples, and the alluring line of chest hair that bisected his chest and belly and then descended to end in a delta at his groin. His gaze followed the line to his cock which overhung two plum-like balls. Cri remembered how long and hard he stared at this resting Adonis before he got a response. How Egon opened his eyes for just a moment, having felt that someone was looking at him, then how he shut them fast from shyness despite the upturned sensuous lips that broke into the slightest shadow of a smile. Cri recalled how he slowly slid across the stone bench towards the object of his lust. How he slowly moved his hand closer and closer to the man's head, with a pounding heart he longed to touch that hair, to feel its silken softness.

He noted how the man seemed to be holding his breath, waiting for that moment of first physical contact and then it happened, Egon reached his hand up over his head as though he were stretching. He let his fingers glance Cri's leg coming to a rest on his thigh. Cri felt the electric shock of the first touch shudder through his body.

"Hello" Cri whispered, "My name is Cri, you are?"

"Egon. This is the first time I have seen you here, yes?"

"True, I usually go to bathe on Haja Street but I heard about this place from a friend."

"You have a friend, a special friend?" Egon asked with some slight trepidation.

"No, do you?"

"No."

"That is good" Cri replied as he moved his hand to rest on Egon's sweat covered chest; his fingers just barely touching his left tit, which he longed to caress more fully.

"We should be careful lest someone come in" Egon said as he sat upright. "Come, let us get some coffee. I live with my parents so we need to go to a street shop. Come on."

"I'm with you."

"How old are you Egon?" Cri asked as he added more sugar to his coffee.

"Twenty-six, you?"

"Twenty-two next month. Do you play soccer? You have really strong legs."

"I used to play a lot but now that I am trying to find work there isn't much time for games."

"I know what you mean. I still play sometimes when I can get away. I work for my old man in his tobacco shop but I hate it so much there. I want to go away. I have some cousins that live in Austria. I would love to go there."

"There is nothing stopping you, why don't you go?"

"Scared a little I guess. Wish I had a friend to go with."

Egon smiled that half smile of his but said nothing though ideas were starting to form in his brain, "Better not get ahead of myself" he thought.

"You live with your parents like me?"

"Yes"

"It is so hard, never time to be alone, to be who you want to be. I so want a place my to be alone... well not alone, like right now. I really like you Egon."

"I like you too Cri. I have a friend that has a little boat, maybe we can take that out sometime if you are free, be alone out on the water for awhile."

"I would love that."

And so their conversation went, tantalizing and full of promise. Cri remembered all the wonderful times they shared. Even the terror they both felt as the packed their bags one night and loaded them into Egon's old truck for the long and dangerous ride into Austria. And now here they were in a damn hospital, Egon with a nasty bump on his head, maybe the police looking into his immigration statues and both of them broke, looking for work. They couldn't stay with Cri's cousin much longer. Something good had to happen. Cri let his head fall forward and tried to snooze.

"Damn these fuckin' Turks to hell" growled Dieter to his comrades as he pressed another two hundred pounds over his head.

Here in the bowels of an abandoned warehouse near the *sudbahnof* where the rumble of trains passing night and day was a constant, Dieter and his friends built themselves a make-shift gym and club house. They had managed to tap into the city power grid giving them some electric light. A broken sofa, a few moth eaten easy chairs, kitchen table and a couple of press benches with bar bells was the extent of their creature comforts except for of course a metal closet that contained a well worn bull whip, an old American style bowie knife, a box full of two and three inch electricians alligator clips, some electric cables, a small World War II field generator, lots of rope, an old German Lugar and their prized possession, a stun gun bought on the black market.

Dieter was the leader. His two and half meter height, massive bi and triceps, perfectly cut pecs and abs sitting on top of rock hard thigh and calf muscles made him a god to his comrades. Dieter kept his pure blond hair cut like an American Marine. He hated the Americans but loved their Marine's look. He often wore military camouflage, military tee shirts and paratrooper boots. Dieter's face was like that of a knight from the Niebelungen Lied with deep piercing blood eyes, pale skin and lantern jaw which he clenched when angry; giving his face the look of an unforgiving brute. His gang loved and feared him in equal measure. His trigger quick temper could change in a second, one moment a hand around a shoulder, another moment a fist in a gut. Dieter kept the allegiance of his troop from fear, intimidation boosted by a generous flow of Euros from extortion, heists and drug running.

The police would bring a few of the gang members in from time to time but Dieter would always show up at the right moment to pay a sergeant or judge off and spring his trooper.

Heinrich, Gus, and Carl sat close together on the old sweat and blood stained sofa passing a joint laced with PCB getting stoned while watching Dieter press iron. He had stripped off his shirt and tee, more to show off his muscled chest than for comfort.

At each press of the bar bells he muttered yet more curses on the head of the Turk that killed his older brother.

"Damn him to hell" was repeated like some mystical hypnotic mantra.

Finally fatigued, Dieter put the bar bell back in the rack, sprung up from the press bench, strode across to his stood compatriots, grabbed the joint from Carl's lips, and stamped it out on the floor.

"Fuck heads, always getting stoned, polluting your bodies with that shit! Now listen to me, find out what hospital that fucking rag head is in and take turns watching him then follow him when he is sprung. I want to know where that fucking shit head lives. You three are going to help me understand, UNDERSTAND!" shouting the last word in their faces.

"Yes Dieter, yes sure thing man" they all answered at once through their clouded brains.

"Then get a fuckin' move in you bastards" he commanded as he yanked the three up by their shirt fronts. "Now get moving."

———————————————

"Well young man, the doctor's say you can go home today. Your friend coming to get you?" asked the nurse.

"Yes Miss, he should be here soon."

"Nice man" she replied as she disconnected his nasal oxygen tube.

"Have you two been friends a long time?"

"About a year now. Miss, did the police say anything or come by, you know, to ask about the accident."

"I just heard it wasn't your fault so you shouldn't worry.

"But what about the other fellow in the car?"

"He died."

"Oh."

"It wasn't your fault. The police said he was drunk and driving very very fast. Now I have to go, take care of yourself."

Left alone Egon got out of bed, dressed and tried to think of some way he and Cri could survive in this city. The last thing they two young men wanted to do was return to Turkey. There was nothing there for them. They might try England but it was hard enough getting in Austria without papers, England would be impossible. Egon sat down on the edge of the bed and stared off into space lost in gloom.

"Egon, here I am. Come on, let's get out of here."

"Cri, what are we going to do?" Now that the police have my name it won't be long before the immigration folks come looking for me. Send me back to Turkey. Cri, I couldn't stand that, being separated from you."

"Don't worry so much. We'll find a way. Come on now, my cousin is waiting in the car; we'll go back to his place and figure out what to do."

"Alright, I'm ready."

As the three men drove out of the parking lot they were unaware that a lone motorbike was close on their tail, even as they drove far out into the immigrant neighborhood the cyclist stayed close behind. When at last the car came to a stop behind a broken down tenement the cyclist slowed down long enough to make a note of the address then sped off back to Dieter.

"Dieter, we found him. He lives with some guy, another Turk, about the same age it looks like. Good strong looking fellow so it might be trouble getting to the driver."

"Shit heads, the three of you can't figure out how to nab two Turks? Figure out a way, bring them both here. Make one watch while we pound the other, two for the price of one as the American's say. I got enough hate in me to take on a dozen, a hundred. Go steal a van, get them the hell here or I'll string the three of you up and put the stunner on your fucking nuts. MOVE!"

shouted Dieter to his easily intimidated henchmen.

The next morning Cri and Egon dressed, drank some strong coffee, and headed out to the streets to spend another day looking for some kind of work. They didn't pay attention to an old white panel truck parked across the street nor did they notice the two leather-clad and helmeted cyclists sitting on their Harley's directly behind the van.

"You two looking for some construction work?" a voice shouted at them from the van's open window.

"Hey you two, I'm Gus, I got some work cleaning a basement in town, interested? Pay you each ten euros."

"Yes, sure" Egon was the first to respond.

"Then get in the back of the van, don't have all day."

As the two opened the back door strong hands pushed the two in and onto the flower. Before they could even struggle, burlap bags were thrown over their heads and their wrists and ankles bound with grey duct tape.

"Get going Heinrich" Gus shouted to the driver as the rear door banged to a close.

Egon and Cri tried to buck loose but the tape held fast. The only thing they could do was lie still and try not to panic.

"You two, we're taking you to Dieter. You know who Dieter is don't you? He's the younger brother of that fellow you killed in your truck. Don't mean to scare you two but Dieter is one hell of a mean son of bitch and he is mighty pissed. You two are going to wish you had never been born. Wishing you were dead before he's finished with you and then again maybe you will" said Gus from the front seat.

Egon and Cri were nearly sick to their stomachs from fear and from the awful stink of the burlap bags that had the distinct smell of urine.

Dieter was just finishing up his preparations for his visitors. He had secured two wooden chairs to the floor and looped four pairs of rope around the cross beams in the basement.

The contents of the grey metal cabinet was neatly arranged on the table. A new roll of silver grey duct tape, a bull whip curled in a perfect loop, the alligator clips lined up in neat rows, the generator and stun gun resting side by side and Lugar within easy reach. Dieter surveyed his arrangement like a painter preparing a still life. He let his fingers caress each instrument of torture lingering on the stun gun which he raised, held before his eyes and pressed the activate button. The thin blue arc buzzed in the stillness like a hornet searching for prey. The sound of the van and two motorcycles driving up behind the building brought a smile to his face.

He stripped off his tee shirt to stand bare chested in wait for the game to begin. He had oiled his chest to better show off his perfectly defined muscles, all the better to terrify his victims. He grabbed the Lugar and caressed it with both hands, holding it up to his face to smell the guns delicious scent of gun oil. What action this gun must have seen during the war he mused for a second. Then Dieter turned to face the door as he heard the stomping booted feet, shouts and muffled grunts as his comrades descended into their basement lair. With a sudden crash the door sprang open vomiting forth two hooded, bound but struggling men followed by they three kidnappers.

"STRIP HIM!" Dieter's two word command was obeyed with much kicking, grabbing, shredding and moaning as Dieter stuck the gun in his waste band. The feel of the cool metal gun handle pressed erotically against his naked side.

Egon and Cri's shirts and pants were soon in shreds, their work boots scattered about the floor, their underwear and tee shirts waded up and thrown in corners. Lastly their burlap bags were removed leaving them temporarily blinded by the harsh overhead bulb that dangled from the ceiling. Before they could start to yell and plead Dieter found their boxers, bunched them up and stuffed them into each of their open mouths.

"Get some tape and secure their gags. Don't want them to scream, they will get the cops on us. Do it." Dieter yelled.

Gus and Heinrich grabbed the roll of duct tape and in minutes had it wound around the men's heads.

"Let me take a look at you two. Damn you Turks all look alike to me. Which is the motherfucker that drove the truck, huh?"

Through their gags they both tried to grunt the word to me but Dieter remembered all to well which one it was. He could never forget Egon's face.

"Don't be trying to protect each other. It was you fucker" he said quietly standing a few inches from Egon. He could feel the heat from Egon's body, see the sweat start to spring from the terrified man's brow, see his labored breathing, his diaphragm clenching in fear.

"Now that it is settled, tie the other one to the chair, this one" indicating Egon. "String up this one up from those ropes over there and get him off the floor, I want to see him swinging."

As Gus, Heinrich and Carl prepared the two captives Dieter returned to the table to retrieve the stun gun. There were three numbered settings on the device, one, two and three. These three innocuous numbers could cause a pure hell of pain and even death if applied to the right part of the body. Dieter played with the switches making the devices sing in ever louder disables, and arc with greater power; the blue flame growing in intensity as each number increased.

The room at last grew silent. Egon's body lifted some two feet off the floor swung gently from the overhead ropes. Cri, arms, legs and ankles bound tightly to the chair sat transfixed at the unfolding horror.

Egon's eyes widened in terror as he watched Dieter; stun gun in hand he moved like a cat tracking a mouse closer and closer. He raised the device and aimed at the young man's dangling ball sack. With a well practiced flick of his wrist he put the setting on number one and just lightly crazed his target. Egon tried to swing his body away from the source but Dieter moved with him, teasing the blue arc against the scrotum.

"Hold him Gus."

"Yes Dieter" Gus said as he positioned himself behind the swinging body. Gus grabbed Egon around the waste, leaned into him with all his weight and nodded to Dieter to proceed.

The gun was turned to level two then placed squarely against his exposed navel.

Even through Egon's gag his desperate scream could be heard. His body bucked and writhed like a wild animal caught in a trap causing for a moment even the stout Gus to nearly loose his balance.

The gun was removed then placed on Egon's right side, again wild bucking and a muffled scream. Sweat streamed down from his face, coating his chest, groins, legs and feet. Drops of perspiration flew across the room as he struggled insanely at each touch of the gun now turned to level three. Dieter aimed next at the circumcised cock head, the blue flame encircling the mushroom head in a torrent of agony.

Cri could be faintly heard as he screamed and pleaded with his captors to show mercy to his friend but his prays were left unanswered. Heinrich, not wanting to be distracted by the sight of such monumental suffering back handed Cri across the face to shut him up. Carl and Heinrich stripped their shirts off sensing the erotic power of the torture. A bulge began to grow between their legs as they stood transfixed by Dieter's magnificent glistening torso and the awesome suffering of the handsome Turk strung up.

At last exhausted by the electric torture and the lack of oxygen Egon's head slumped forward and he fell into a blessed comma.

"Wake him Gus" Dieter hissed as he returned the stun gun to the table.

"You two get this alligator clips and clamp them to his tits, cock and balls, turn him into porcupine."

Tears could be seen streaming down Cri's face as he sat struggling in his bondage chair. The duct tape was too much to break through, he knew this but try he must. How could men do such things to others he kept asking himself, how?

Gus, who always kept a stash of cheap beer in the basement

opened a can, strode across to the naked man and splashed the contents into Egon's face and across his chest.

Slowly the young man came back to his agony, noticing first the burning around his wrists where the rope had dug mercilessly into his flesh, leaving his hands frozen from lack of blood flow, unable to move his fingers he felt a new terror that he might never be able to use his hands again, if he survived.

Heinrich and Carl, each with a handful of the electrician's alligator clamps began their decorating. The razor sharp jaws bit like hornets into Egon's tits sending tiny streams of blood from their teeth to run down his chest. Other clips were placed around the head of Egon's cock then down each side of his shaft while the remaining instruments of torture were firmly clamped onto his battered ball sack. When at last their handy work was complete, the two stepped away to admire the sight. Dieter, bull whip in hand snapped the raw hide in the air a few times as he moved to stand some ten feet from his target.

"Let me see how many strokes it will take to whip off these clips, any bets? What, there are thirty on their. What do you Gus, Heinrich, Carl, you?" as he turned to look at Cri's tear stained face.

"Move back now, give me room."

The three others didn't have to be asked twice. They all leaned against the far wall with eager anticipation.

The whip snapped in the air three times just so Dieter could get a feel for the room and the space needed to hit his target. Egon swung helplessly from the ropes, two exhausted to force his body into a swing that is until the first contact of whip against a clip that was biting into his right tit... The leather tip of the whip snagged the spring of the alligator clip and tore free from the nipple leaving a bit of ragged flesh in its wake.

Egon nearly choked from the unimaginable pain emanating across his chest and into his gut. His eyes nearly popped from their sockets. He twisted and tried to swing away from Dieter but to no available as the next arc of the whip landed on his left nipple causing yet more hellish agony, again lacerating the tip as the razor teeth ripped through the tender flesh. Again and again the whip landed with passion alternating between the left and right nipple, keeping up a rhythm of leather against flesh. A muffled scream followed by another crack, scream and another. Dieter's powerful muscles, coated with sweat glowed in the overhead light making him look like some magnificent demon from hell, torturing some lost sinner in the fiery depths. Once the tits were free Dieter took aim at his victims cock and balls. The whip cut into the tender flesh, adding to the dreadful rending of the clips as they tore free turning his once proud manhood into a mass of cuts and bruises, swelling at each blow and into something more horrible then could be imagined. He still struggled and swung in the air, hardly able to comprehend the ghastly all consuming stinging like thousands of swarming wasps that seemed to consume his entire body. At last nature intervened. His head fell forward into blessed oblivion.

"Well done Dieter."

"Very good work."

"Yes that was great, have a beer Dieter, you must be thirsty?" offered Gus.

But Dieter brushed them all aside. He was now a man possessed by some horrific demon. He stormed over to the table and grabbed the hand generator and two long wire cables that had been stripped of insulation some two inches at one end and a foot at the other. He dragged a spare chair across the room and positioned it before the hanging body and placed the generator on the seat. Next he deftly wound one end of copper wire around the base of Egon's cock, the other around his bloody balls, and attached to wires to the generator's posts.

Grabbing Gus's beer he splashed the suds across his victim's body and face reviving him once again.

"Bring me something to sit on" Dieter said full of controlled menace.

"That stool will do," he said pointing to the corner.

Cri started to pray, any god that might hear him, he begged for his friend, his lover to be saved. Almost more then he could bare he sobbed through his gag, his shoulders and chest shuddering in spasms of despair.

Dieter sat down on the stool, positioned his hands firmly on the crank and looked up at Egon whose head was inclined downwards. The two men locked eyes, boring into each other's souls. Dieter with all the malice that one human could feel for another, Egon with all the lost hope that man can feel when faced with what he knew would be his final agony.

"This is for my Wilhelm you bastard," Dieter screamed at the top of his lungs as he began to slowly turn the crank. The electric power began as a slight tingle then grew and grew and grew into a burning crushing rending of Egon's manhood. His body arched wildly nearly snapping in two from the unfathomable pain. His head snapped back and forth, his eyes squeezed tight as though by not seeing he could somehow blot out the pain. Sweat again poured forth from his twisting body spraying like some garden sprinkler across the room. Gus, Heinrich and Carl, each with growing hadrons' unzipped their flies and began to stroke their rigid poles. And Cri? Cri wept more bitter tears.

It was the sound of police sirens approaching that gave the assembly pause.

"What the fucking hell?" Dieter yelled, stopping the crank.

"Were you two followed, did anyone see you bring them here? Shit heads, what the fuck?" But before any answers could be given the basement door smashed open, shattered by a police battering ram. Police with guns drawn filled the room, herding the four goons up against the wall as Cri's cousin following the cops ran to untie first his relative then the two bounded up and gently lowered Egon to the floor. Cri felt a knife in his chest from fear that his lover was dead but the intervention of an attending medic confirmed that he was still breathing.

It took a month for Egon to recover in hospital. As soon as he was well enough he was deported back to Turkey to join Cri who had been sent out of country within days of the raid. The two found work as sheep herders far up in the hills where they are today living out their lives and trying to forget Dieter and Vienna.

Mister Naldini

"Mister Naldini wants to see you boy. We gotta car waitin' outside so get a move on."

Bruno, in a thick Brooklyn accent, shouted these chilling words into Tony's right ear, trying to be heard over the riotous drunken laugher from the denizens of the Blue Note, Asbury Park's most notorious speak easy.

Tony polished off his shot of cheap scotch in one gulp, put the glass down, grabbed his coat and muffler, and followed Bruno out into the ragging Northeaster that was pounding the Jersey coast. The black rain drenched the 31 LaSalle that sat idling in the dank alley beside the bar, its motor softly purring. Tony, whose heart started to pound like a base drum in a marching band, could just make out the shadowy figures of the driver and two forms sitting in the rear seat. Something wasn't right and he knew it. He glanced over his shoulder as he sought some escape route but Bruno's hulking frame loomed too close behind for Tony to make a run for it.

The right rear door opened, a hand holding a Saturday night special motioned for him to climb in.

"Get in, ain't got all night. Don't wanna keep Mr. Naldini waitin' do we?" Bruno said as he pushed Tony into the back where he was wedged between two Neanderthals.

In an instant Bruno slammed his three hundred and fifty

pounds into the front passenger seat, the rear door was closed and locked and the car sped off towards the open road.

Tony figured they were heading south, maybe towards Atlantic City.

"Bruno, fellas, what's this all about. How come Naldini wants to see me?"

The man on Tony's left, whose face was hidden by a scarf and low placed Fedora jabbed a gun in Tony's left side and muttered, "You'll find out soon enough."

"Better just keep my mouth shut" thought the now terrified captive as he tried to sit back and relax. How the hell had he gotten himself into this mess? Damn, he was only twenty-four, smart, good lookin', or so Hal had told him. He sure missed Hal. That's it he thought, think about Hal. Whenever I think of my buddy Hal I get a boner and can't think of nothin' else. Get my mind off this situation. Damn, there is some kind of mistake, a misunderstanding. Maybe Mr. Naldini has a special job for me to do. I done that last shipment of booze outta Canada and down here to Asbury, nice and easy, not a bottle lost. That's it; Mr. Naldini has a job for me. Maybe make some real money this time. Go out to California, me and Hall, get a little boat, be real happy Hal and me. God Hal was good lookin', football captain, all the girls crazy about him in high school. He could have had his pick but he picked me, me just a bench warmer. Me, I was good at swimin'. Hal always came to the natatorium in Ocean Grove to watch me. He tried to visualize every inch of his buddy's body, recall his soft wavy wheat colored hair, sky blue eyes, the perfectly muscled shoulders and that chest, like some sculpture guy in a museum or something. He squeezed his eyes shut real hard and conjured up the image of the two of them lying on the beech in Belmar. Tony, all bronzed, thick pelt of hair on his chest, soft black hair against the peaches and cream color of Hal's skin... and then there was Tony's prick, all long and white with a head like a wild growin' mushroom that he loved to take in his mouth. The four years since they left high school, workin' odd jobs, walkin' the boardwalk, fuckin' on the beech, those were mighty fine times. Of course sometimes Hal disappeared for sometimes weeks, no explanation. Just some work on the road he would say. Tony did his own disappearing acts, running booze from Canada on small boats that landed off Manasquan or Point Pleasant in the dark of night, working for Mr. Naldini. And then both flush with money the two of them would hop a train from Asbury and go into the city, take in the Follies or some such thing or dinner at Delmonicos like two swells. Sometimes they would check out one of the all men's bar down in the Village were two lads were allowed to hold hands and maybe even dance together. Tony's mind wondered further as he tried to imagine that the two of them were entwined in each other's arms on a blanket under the boardwalk. He tried to feel that smooth warm flesh that covered those steel cable muscles, the taste of Hal's skin as Tony teased his lover's nipples with his tongue or bit down hard on the perfectly formed rose bud man nips, ah he felt a warm glow in his crotch but, between the constant banging of the windshield wipers, the pounding of the rain and the jab of the gun barrel in his rib cage the fiery images soon faded into the cold dank blackness of the back seat

Damn, if this is a job, something good, then why the gun? Alright, just take deep breaths, wait and see, wait and see.

After endless hours driving over rain slicked roads twisting and turning deep into the Jersey pine barrens, Bruno broke the terrifying silence.

"Turn left and down dat dirt road then pull up by da gate."

The LaSalle bounced along the deeply rutted road for another ten minutes as the pelting rain and wind lashed at the car. With a sudden stop, the passengers lurched forward as Bruno oozed his fat frame out of the car and opened the barb wire fence allowing the car to pass. Once the auto cleared the gate, Bruno returned to the car and they drove on in.

Damn, I sure don't like this one bit Tony thought as he strained to see out the mud and rain spattered windows. Where the hell are we he thought; and like magic, the headlights caught in their glare the side of a well worn barn, and broken down farm house. In the drive were six or seven other drenched and mud coated cars. Lined up like a funeral cortège waitin' on the body.

"Pull up right in front of those double doors." Bruno gave the instruction and was silently obeyed.

"Bruno, come on, you gotta tell me what this is all about." Tony tried not to sound too scared but there was now a distinct quiver in his voice.

"Listen here Tony," Bruno said as he turned to the back and faced the wide eyed captive. "Mr. Naldini got some questions he's gonna ask ya and if you know what's good for ya and want to keep that pretty boy body of yours in one fuckin' piece, you answer him real honest. Then maybe he gonna let ya go or put ya outta your misery fast like but believe you me, he think you lien to him or not telling everythin' you know, he make you wish you never been born. We also got a buddy of yours, nice big surprise from Mr. Naldini, a little company; misery loves company, that's why Ma used to say." Bruno laughed a little at his tiny jest.

My God thought Tony. What the hell?

The other men in the car who had not uttered a word these many hours grunted in agreement to Bruno's sage advice.

"Now come on, get outta the car."

With one man on each elbow, heads bowed against the pelting onslaught of rain, wind and flying leaves the four men made their way through the mud and pot holes to the barn.

Bruno with his ham sized fist banged sharply on the door which in a few moments slowly creaked open all of two inches. A sliver of a face could be seen talking to Bruno: that was all Tony could see then. Damn, he had to piss, he was scared shitless. After a few more words passed through the crack one side of the double doors begin to creak on its rusted hinges opening onto a scene that knocked Tony's breath right out of his lungs. There, dangling some two feet off the stinking straw covered floor was his pal, Hal. His wrists were tied by thick nasty hemp rope which was wound tight over a cross beam high up in the barn's roof. His shirt was shredded with barely enough fabric to cover his naked chest. Hal's head was down, resting on his chin, a livid black eye and a trickle of blood ran down from the corners of his mouth. He was still breathing, that Tony could tell as his but was stretched so tight and smooth that the slightest inhalation registered.

His paints were mud stained and torn but still managed to hold to his waist.

Tony's eyes nearly popped out of his head. Jesus Christ, what the hell was all this about he wondered, his vision like through a tunnel as his gaze bore in at the horrible sight but a sharp push from Bruno an his goons towards the center of the barn made him aware of other almost equally alarming sights.

Two pallid overhead electric lights cast garish shadows on the walls, like some Asbury Park fun house room.

Sitting at a small paint chipped table was the wizened old Mr. Naldini himself, dressed impeccably as he always was in a tailor made three piece pin strip suit. His white spats could be seen topping his shoes beneath the table. Lying in wait for further use was a pair of electric cables and an old fashioned field generator, some relic from the First World War, next to a well worn bull whip that was neatly coiled like some waiting cobra.

Scattered around the room were at least a dozen other men seated in a variety of half broken wooden chairs or lounging on bales of moldy hay all facing Hal as though his dangling body were some ghoulish performance or living sculpture. The old men in the barn delighted in seeing the young Adonis stretched and helpless. He became a focal point for their rage at growing old, for their hatred of their fellow man and mostly for themselves. Of course there were a few of the men who were obviously enjoying the spectacle of the handsome blond lad strung up before them. More then one thug, with raincoat draped over his lap, a hand discreetly resting between wide spread legs, a thin film of sweat on the upper lip stared hungrily in high expectation of things yet to come. The other's looked either bored or disgusted by Naldini's cruelty, silently asking if they had anything in their pasts that might lead them to similar treatment. The risks of leading a gangster life were pretty considerable, a thought that buzzed around more then a few of the assembled mugs heads. The trick was to always get in the first punch, show no mercy, dog eat dog, and stay on top.

"Buona Sera Tony, amici mea." Naldini oozed charmingly as he stood to great the young man.

"We are so, how you say, delighted you could join us on such a stormy night. I see from your big eyes staring that you know our other guest? Boys, bring Tony on in, get a chair for this fine young fella. It is so warm in here, STRIP HIM." Naldini shouted the final two word order with all the venom he could muster. "And tie him good and tight to the chair, don't want him falling off, might hurt himself, eh?" he said to the assembled audience.

"Right away Mr. Naldini." Salvatore, Naldini's right hand man, always ready and happy to use his muscle or his trigger finger, whatever was called for marched right up to Tony who was held tight by the double escort. With well practiced mitts Sal yanked off the boys coat, ripped the shirt and shredded his white tee shirt and had him slammed down into a waiting ladder back chair. From out of nowhere several ropes were produced, one to tie Tony's hands behind his back, one to hitch around his chest, the rope digging painfully just below his nipples and one long rope to tie his ankles firmly to the legs of the seat. And all the while he was being trussed up the petrified young man stared wild eyed at his friend who still hung limply from the overhead beam. Tony was hardly able to breathe, his heart beating a wild tattoo, his brow, chest and hands cold and clammy with fear sweat. God damn, what was going to happen to Hal, to him. What the hell was all this about.

"Mr. Naldini Sir, I don't understand."

"Shut the hell up, wait till Mr. Naldini speaks" barked Sal as he back handed the captive across the mouth. Tony saw stars and for a second lost the sense of where he was and what was happening but the bitter taste of blood in his mouth soon brought him back to his senses.

"Sal, get some water and wake the other one up."

"Yes, boss."

"Now Tony, Bruno tells me you and this other piece of meat hangin' here are, finnochio, fairies. What you gotta' say to that Tony? Ain't no room in my organization for no fruits but that is neither here nor there at the moment. Bruno also tells me that you boys are actually workin' for the Feds. What you gotta say about that Anthony?"

"What? That's' a lie Mr. Naldini. Hal and me, we're just two guys tryin' to make a little money. We'd never work for no coppers no how Mr. Naldini. Bruno is liein'. You gotta believe me."

"Hmmmm, well Bruno tells me you got contacts all over the shore. I want their names. I also learned dat you know where the Carlucci family is off loadin' some prime Irish whiskey next week. You gonna tell me where and when that drop is takin' place?"

"I swear to God Mr. Naldini Hal and me, we ain't cops and know nothing about the Carlucci's. You gotta believe me."

"Sal" Mr. Naldini spoke softly yet in that one word, Salvatore knew what the next step.

Naldini stepped out of the way as the buck of icy water was thrown at Hal's dangling body. With a short sharp gasp and violent shaking of his mane, Hall came back to life.

"Ah, my boy Hal, I hope you had a pleasant rest. You see we brought your friend Anthony to keep you company. Since you two fruits are so sweet on one another perhaps watching each other will loosen one of your tongues. Besides, sadly as it pains me to say, you two are here be made examples of lest any of you other mugs sitting out there even think of turning fruity or worst yet playin' both ends against the middle and workin' for the feds.

Sal, strip off this fellas pants and boxers. Let's see what is so appealin' to Mr. Tony here."

Hal tried to swing out of the way but Sal's fist to his lower abdomen cut short any further flailing about. Sal quickly yanked the dangling man's shoes off, then with a mighty yank left the poor fellow stark naked. His cock and balls having receded into his groin from fear left him feeling more ashamed and naked then he had ever felt before. His face glowed crimson, so easy to see through his fine white skin. Anthony was frozen in terror for his friend as he watched helplessly the next part of the ordeal. Sal took the two wire cables each ending in shiny razor sharp teeth and attached one onto Hal's scrotum. The other he pinched tight on the shaking man's inner thigh some five inches below his dangling dick. A few tiny pin pricks of blood dripped from the alligators penetrating bite. Hal felt like two giant hungry wasps had landed between his legs. He struggled to overcome the pain and the fear that now gripped his gut for he saw Sal attach the other ends of the cables to the two posts protruding from the top of the field generator. Sweat poured off his brow, momentarily blinding him as it the salty fluid invaded his eyes. A quick shake of his head and sweat drops flew across the barn. Tony's jaw dropped open as he watched the preparations.

"Mr. Naldini, please Sir. Hal ain't done anything wrong. We ain't coppers. I don't know what the hell Bruno was tellin' ya but its all damn lies, damn lies."

"Sal, turn the crank, show these two meat balls what's in store for 'em."

Sal placed his hands on the crank, the gears engaged, the magneto began to turn, the power wended its way from the guts of the machine through the wire into the Hals groin.

It was a slow tingle at first, almost a tickle at first. Had Hal's wrists and shoulder's been in such agony he might almost just almost found it slightly pleasurable but then Sal turned the crank a little faster, the magneto spun more rapidly, more juice flowed through the cable, the alligator clips seemed to tighten, digging deeper into the soft flesh of thigh and balls sack. Hal's body began to vibrate as though from some awful bout of fever. He clamped his jaw shut as tight as possible, shut his eyes, clenched his fists, and still, the stinging burning sensation flowed ever on causing his muscles in his crotch, legs, and abdomen to clench ever so tighter and painful. The crank turned faster and faster, sweat dripping down his face, his torso now drenched with per-spiration that dripped like rain drops onto the straw floor between his dangling body.

"Stop, stop damn you all, Stop," Tony pleaded with all his might.

"Sal" and with the one word from Mr. Naldini the crank came to a holt.

Hal, exhausted hung like the proverbial drenched dish rag. He tried to take in great gulps of air but the weight of his body and the strain on his rib cage prevented all but the shallowest of breaths.

"Now Anthony, Tony that is, that was just a taste of what Sal can do to your friend. Come on fillio mio give us the names of your contacts. As you see your friends here have nothing better to do, don't want to go driving around in this storm so here we all are enjoyin' the show. You tell, give us some names and the dope on the Carlucci family, we give you fruits a good wippin' maybe we let you go. What do you say Tony?"

"Mr. Naldini, sir, I swear to God and Virgin Mary that we are not cops, feds, nothin'. We just wanted to make a few bucks bringin' in some booze. You've been lied to Mr. Naldini. Please believe me. Bruno, you know, you are lying about this. You know Hal and me, we ain't snitches.

"Sal" Naldini nodded to his henchmen, "String this one up beside his friend."

Hearing these words Hal lifted up his head and watched in

disbelief as Tony was untied from his chair and stripped naked."

"Sal, hang this one from his ankles, makes a better target for the whip."

Sal enlisted two other most willing members from the "audience" to assist. Tony received a swift hard kick to his nuts that doubled him over in pain. In a second his assailants had him flat on the ground while ropes were tied to his ankles, the rope end tossed over the cross beam and with many a grunt and groan from Sal he was lifted off the ground dangling free up side down next to his pal. Like a swinging piece of prime beef his powerful well honed muscular body was displayed naked for all to see. And what a sight it was. Tony was nicknamed the Cavello the horse in high school for the size of his manhood. His prick was long and fat and his balls were like two large peaches in size. A thick forest of black hair could not hide their size and heft. His chest, matted now in sweat and his belly were pulled taught in a most exciting way. His powerful calves and thighs strained under the weight of his torso. The cruel rope burnt into the flesh of his ankles causing agonizing pain in his feet.

The blood rushed to his face turning it red like a setting sun in summer.

"Sal" another one word command from Naldini and the whip was brought from the table to be unfurled and snapped in mid air.

"Begin Sal"

Sal took his place some ten feet behind the naked dangling man and with the expertise of a Texas wrangler struck the first blow. The bull whip sliced through the air with a whistle and landed across the naked ass and back. Tony's eyes nearly bulged out of his head at the suddenness and sharpness of the fire like mark.

"You can stop this Anthony, you can stop this Hal."

No response from either man was forthcoming.

"Sal, lay it on."

"With pleasure Mr. Naldini."

And so the whip was raised and whistled and found its mark. This time a few inches caressed the young man's scrotum. He let out a terrible shriek like some high pitched scream from a stuck pig. The goons in the barn all broke out in applause and laughter as the whip whistled again and again crisscrossing the back, ass and groin with blood dripping rivers of agony. At each lash, Hal, in unison with his lover Tony, screamed curses at Naldini and the pitiless spectators. After twenty lashes Tony hung limp, passed out from the overwhelming pain.

"Bruno, come here." Mr. Naldini beckoned the ox to come forward.

"Yes Mr. Naldini." Bruno sheepishly replied.

"You sure you not telling me stories about this two fellas? I'm startin' to wonder why they would not be talking."

"That's easy Sir, they know if they talk you'll blow 'em away."

"Maybe you should be the one we string up and put the wires on? Can't see wastin' munch more time on these two. Sal, cut 'em down and take 'em in the back, bury 'em good and deep, don't want no dogs diggin' this two fruit cases up. Now let this be a lesson to the rest of you. You even think of talking to the cops or worse turning into fags, see what happens to you." Naldini said all this while staring hard at Bruno. He knew Bruno was lying through his teeth. Probably the dumb ass had feelings for one of these two fellas. Didn't matter. He had made his point, wasted a couple of no good fruits for the edification of his mob and in particular, Bruno.

Sal and several of the assembly lowered the exhausted young men to the ground. Hal and Tony looked at each other in utter disbelief at their fate. They had done nothing but love each other and help with some small time gin running and now this.

"Come on you two, stand up, time to meet your maker" said Sal with a sneer.

"Sal" Mr. Naldini called as he pulled a knife from his pocket and handed it to his executioner. "Geld 'em before you shoot 'em. Nothin' makes me sicker then fruits."

"Me too boss. Get a move on you two. We gonna do this nice and slow. Hold 'em down boys, spread their legs good and wide."

Hal and Tony screamed with all their might as though their voices could pierce the raging storm outside and find its way to God's ears. The assembled mobsters all rushed to the front of the barn and with greedy hands held the two wildly struggling men down on the floor. Their rough hands dug into the men's arms and legs and Ton and Hal fought with all their might to escape.

"Noooooooooo." The both cried in unison as Sal grabbed first Hal's ball sack, pulled it up and away from his splayed crotch and sliced in one quick movement. Then with lighting speed, Tony's balls were in the Sal's fist, yanked up and out and the blade sliced through the skin.

"Damn these two sure can bleed."

"Get it over with, makes me sick." Naldini ordered as he and his gang made their way out into the cold unforgiving night. Two shots could be heard over the raging storm.

Rack and Repent

I, Clarence of Dunwich Abbey, do offer the following account to you, Most Reverend Father Thomas, Abbot of Dunwich Abbey, of my most grievous sins against my fellow man, the Sacred Realm of England, and Holy Mother, the Church. Be it known that I offer up this document of my treason and wanton cruelty, not in the hope of Salvation before the Throne of God, but as a warning to others who may read these words as a dread warning against pride, envy, and blood lust.

It was in the year of Our Lord Thirteen Hundred and Forty-Eight, as the great pestilence ravaged the land, when bodies both high- and low-born were piled like cordwood in tumbrels to be carted off to common stinking pits and covered with lime, that I first saw William of Preston. He had come to our family's Castle on the cruel windswept coast of Suffolk as an Ambassador from Edward III, to enlist our help in the King's feud with John of Somerset. I remember as if it were but a moment ago, standing on the parapet, my falcon perched on my arm, watching the young Knight and his retainers gallop with such resolution up the road leading to our drawbridge. How the sun gleamed off his breastplate, dazzling my senses. His helmet's visor was up. I could see his strong jaw coated in dark stubble from a fortnight's want of shaving. His dark eyes with their fixed gaze focused on the road and the drawbridge and nothing else. It was a look of total concentration and resolution. His magnificent shoulders, encased as they were in finely wrought armor, were like some pagan god's. His thighs were like the finest supple elm trees supported by calves of such perfect contours that my very breath caught in my throat. He appeared, from my high vantage point, to be nothing save the very incarnation of a heaven-sent angel or fiend, I knew not which. I had naught before felt such a thrill at the sight of another human being in all my twenty-four years. Oh, yes, I confess that stable lads or rough but comely peasants from the land's surrounding our domain had thrilled me and tempted me to lust and to brandish a whip while in a colic or playful mood but this was some new sensation. Some overriding passion seized my heart and loins, blurring all other considerations.

As the Knight passed into the outer courtyard below me, I quickly turned, passed my ravenous falcon, Hermes, to my bumbling page and dashed with all haste down the parapet steps. I had to find out who this man was and what brought him to our Castle. By the time I reached the bottom step William was dismounting from his magnificent black stallion. He removed his helmet and handed it to a stable boy at the ready. Then I could see the true perfection of his face. His head was crowned with a full head of light auburn hair the color of a warm autumn afternoon. A high fine forehead, thick, dark and full eyebrows, cheekbones of such perfection to make Apollo jealous, lips of perfect fullness and color, which smiled with warmth to make Norse ice melt into a spring stream. Such beauty of body and, I assumed, such perfection of spirit gave me a feeling of falling into some dark agony. I felt such a longing to possess this paragon of manhood, to penetrate him bodily and spiritually, all this from but a few minutes in his presence. Had I been overtaken by the Devil himself I could not have felt so strong a compulsion to capture and rend this young god. But I must bide my time. By his Royal standard I knew that he would be a formidable challenge but one that I would subdue in good time. As I stood transfixed, my father's secretary scampered into the chilly inner courtyard with a squad of Castle guards to escort the young envoy into my father's most august presence. As usual I knew I would be excluded from the audience chamber. The most powerful tyrant that ruled over our county with a fist of iron had little time for me, his only son and heir. I knew full well that he had no intention of leaving the land or Castle to me but was actively trying to sire another son from any number of Castle wenches. But I digress. The fact is that I was not welcome. This in itself was no obstacle as I had long ago seduced one of the Castle scribes. McGregor was his name, and his sole purpose in life, as far as I was concerned, was to serve me as my eyes and ears at court. He hailed from the wilds of Scotland. A man of some twenty and three years, he was short with a full mane of curly red hair that crowned a face of surpassing beauty. His deep hazel eyes were filled with fire and longing for life, a fact that I relied on. He had a barrel chest with the finest pair of nipples that peaked like spring rose buds so enchantingly against his snow-white flesh. I was constantly at pains not to damage those enchanting nubs too much and so deprive myself of another night's delicious agony and delight. Oh I had pinched, bit, and burned with taper wax those alluring points of delight as he struggled, spread-eagled in my chamber or better yet, to take him into the woods on a hunting expedition only there to strip him naked, spread him between some stout oak trees and wale away at his magnificent back and chest with a variety of whips and scourges that I kept in my saddle bags.

How glorious it was to note each lash mark across that gorgeous naked body. The fair skin was a perfect pallet for me to work my art. Never mind you, enough to cause him permanent damage, for he was too perfect a young buck for that, but rather to leave him with the proper respect for my position. He knew that these beatings were a warning that should he ever betray me or fail me in any way, these lashings would be but a hint of the agony to follow. It had taken but a brief visit to the dank cold dungeon room, a cursory look at the instruments of torture and death, that the young fellow swore total allegiance to my person. The racks, both horizontal and vertical, with their well-worn ropes dangling from pulleys, the spiked iron chair with the drawer beneath the seat for burning coals, the pear which could be heated to glowing red and whose petals when inserted in a man's bung hole could be opened ever so slowly. Then there were the banks of whips, scourges and flails, blood- and sweat-stained, that hung from the chamber's walls. So many devices that had been brought to our Castle over the years, all for the express purpose of instilling terror in any man that would think of challenging the accepted order of Dunwich Castle. I could tell from the look of fear in McGregor's eyes that he knew full well that he would be fair game to be burned with irons or that his nipples would be thrust through with thick iron needles to be used as suspension points, taking his entire body's weight, but again good Father Abbot, I stray from my point. You see how my poor beleaguered mind does roam from time to time.

I followed William and his retinue as far as the antechamber to the great hall. There, two of my father's more gruesome guards crossed their gleaming halberds across the portal, preventing me from following the object of my desire. A courtier slammed the door and I could tell by the sound of heavy wood sliding on iron that the bolt was locked into place. This must be a high level and secret meeting. Fortunately McGregor had been called to record the business at hand so I had naught to do but bide my time. Taking a seat on a cold stone bench I began to while away the time with plots and plans for capturing my prey.

But my reverie was interrupted by Sir Robert Holland who sat down next to me with some delightful news. Sir Robert, though still engaged as captain of the Castle guard, was, unbeknownst to my father, his bitterest enemy. Robert had over the years lost the affections of his wife, whom, I might add, he loved mostly for her dowry, to his liege lord. In our mutual hate we shared one other common interest: the sight, sound, and smell of men in torment. Holland was in an ideal position to exercise his passion, charged as he was to maintain security. It fell to him to interrogate suspected traitors, tax evaders, and thieves. Whenever a particularly interesting victim fell into his claws he was sure to alert me. He enjoyed taking turns on the myriad instruments of torture in the dungeon and, if I don't flatter myself too much, what better partner than I.

"My Lord, forgive me for interrupting, but we have apprehended a farmer from the shire who dared to poach on your good father's land. He is being taken to the dungeon this very moment for some suitable punishment. I thought perhaps, had you nothing better to do, that you might like to join me?"

Well, dear Abbot, you can imagine my enthusiastic response.

"Kind, thoughtful Sir Robert, I would be enchanted. Lead the way and as we walk describe the young fellow. I rely on your good taste in these matters."

"Well, Clarence, the man's name is Hal. He is perhaps thirty-two or -three. The miscreant is a tall robust fellow with a fine dark brown beard, a handsome sun-bronzed face. He looks to have a powerful chest and back and tree trunk legs. Years spent behind a plow and lifting bales has given him what appears to be a splendid set of muscles. And most importantly he has plenty of the devil's own spirit. He struggled like a wild boar as my men netted him in the forest. Found with a brace of quail in his sack, caught with the goods, as my men would say. They said that even once he was tied hand and foot he bucked and writhed so that it took all their strength to lift him up and place a stout pole between his bindings. Carted him off like a fine piece of game, they did. I told my men to hold off stripping him till we arrive. There is nothing like the total humiliation from a slow stripping and rending of a man's garments before his betters, now is there, Clarence? I am also intrigued to gain a sight of his manhood. Judging from my men's account he appears to have a fine pouch of meat between his legs. But come, good Sir, we are almost here."

Holland had a fine way with words. I could feel a warm glow in my balls that began to emanate in ever widening circles throughout my body. If I could not yet possess the young Knight, this peasant sounded like a reasonable appetizer.

When Sir Robert and I arrived in the dungeon, Hal was still hogtied and lay on the filthy straw-strewn floor. Even after the hours of his journey he remained unbowed. He fought the cruel rough ropes binding his wrists and ankles with all his strength, hoping, as it were, to wear them down and somehow free himself. Foolish man he was, for even had he loosened the ties, where was he to go? His wild trashing had loosened and torn his grey peasant shirt, revealing luxurious chest hair covering his obviously finely sculpted chest. I longed to grab the front of his shirt and with my very fists slowly rip the fabric to shreds but Robert's hand on my shoulder cautioned me against being over zealous.

"Let him toil some more. Is it not fine to watch such manly prowess toil in vain against his bonds?"

I agreed most heartily and so we took ourselves to a rough wooden bench and made ourselves comfortable. The prisoner went on with his exertions but soon was overcome with fatigue. Now only mumbling pleas for mercy, peppered with mention of starving wife and babes, to say nothing of the occasional curse against us and God alike, he soon wore himself to exhaustion.

"Now, perhaps, Robert, we should introduce ourselves?"

"I most heartily agree, good My Lord. Perhaps a dousing of some cold water to bring him back to his senses might be in order. Let me fetch some from the guards." Robert was as good as his word and with speed departed the dungeon. Alone with the prisoner, I stood and stomped towards the prisoner. With his arms and legs tied behind, his back arched, his chest and belly bowed forward made a perfect target for my heavily booted foot, which I planted with a swift kick aimed at this gut. The toe of my boot met strong resistance. His belly was firm, drum-like, though the suddenness and force of my punt did knock his breath away.

"Ah, good peasant, you are awake," I said as I planted my foot between his legs. With slow and deliberate moves I found his groin. I could feel even through my boot his prodigious man-hood. Then finding better purchase I began to press the toe of my boot down onto his crotch. He tried in vain to slide away, but my foot followed, ever increasing the pressure, mashing through his worn trousers his very manhood. Just then the dungeon grate swung open and Robert appeared with his bucket of frigid water.

"Step aside, Clarence; our peasant looks thirsty." And with those words, with one bounding movement a cascade of freezing liquid drenched the hapless prisoner. "There now, wash a little stink off this rustic fellow. Come now, let's lift him up and have a better look."

Hal sputtered and shook his head from side to side like a drenched dog as we grabbed him from under his arms. With practiced skill I untied his legs long enough to yank his panta-loons down to his ankles. His homespun linen drawers followed next. I nearly gasped at the sight. His buttocks were total per-fection. High, gleaming white orbs of such power and grace were a sight to behold, but then I caught sight of his manhood. Like an Arabian stallion, he was hung with two fine orbs and a thick, though not over-long cock. A fine patch of dark brown hair crowned his rod and softly enveloped his balls. I could not keep my hands from him. I grasped with my right hand his sack and felt the delicious weight of his jewels. Such heft they had while encased in such velvety soft flesh. He gasped at the intrusion on his person but before he could protest too much, Robert and

I, with all due speed, encumbered though Hal was by fabric binding his legs, dragged him to the center of the room where chains and iron cuffs dangled tantalizingly from the vaulted ceiling. Robert, an expert with a rope, re-bound his wrists, securing them tightly. Standing before the now wildly struggling prisoner, Holland planted his fat fist into the peasant's abdomen, momentarily stilling him. Just long enough it was to remove his pants and under garments and secure his ankles to the black iron rings imbedded into the stone floor. With his legs now spread like a wishbone from a giant bird, his manhood dangled invitingly before our eyes.

"So, Sir Robert, tell us, what is the punishment for poaching on the Liege Lord's estate?" I inquired, knowing full well what harsh treatment the law prescribed.

"Why, Sir, it is a hundred lashes and a brand, that all may see the miscreant for a poacher and thief."

"Let us proceed then. Shall I go first?" said I smiling as I walked to the row of whips and flails, taking my time at choosing just the right one. I did not want to start with anything too damaging, not just yet, at any rate. I chose a fine braided whip of some considerable length and heft. The high vaulted ceiling allowed for a full extension of the leather, allowing the wielder great flexibility. I always enjoyed snapping a whip to make the prisoners jump before the actual landing of rawhide against naked human flesh. I planted myself well behind that perfectly muscled back, stretched bulging shoulder muscles glistening from the cold sweat of dread. A few more loud cracks, like the first part of lightening before the rumble of thunder, jolted into Hal's brain. And then I struck the first sudden lacerating sting across his outstretched back, slicing ever so delicately but excruciatingly into his senses. There was the powerful intake of air, the surprise at the intensity of the pain, then followed a cry, high-pitched it was, more a yelp, come to think of it. But of course this was just the beginning. Some ninety-nine were to follow. And at each blow of the whip, I increased the intensity, crisscrossing that contoured canvas with a road map of angry red welts trickling blood and sweat. Eventually his screams grew more ferocious. His body draped forward as far as the chains would allow, his toes barely able to find purchase on the slick stones beneath his over-arched body. I could see from the corner of my eye Sir Robert sitting on the bench with legs wide apart, his hand firmly planted between his legs, messaging his obviously growing cock. At last my fifty strokes were complete, much to my chagrin I might add. Time it was for me to hand over the whip to Sir Robert. As I turned to hand off the whip to Holland, McGregor appeared at the chamber grate.

"My Lord, the council meeting is concluded. The King's emis-sary has retired to his chamber for the night. I thought you might like to know," McGregor said with the slightest hint of a smirk on his handsome face.

"Very well, I will follow you and leave Sir Robert to finish the work at hand." And so saying I left the dungeon, trying somewhat half-heartedly to disguise the tumescence in my loins, for the thrashing of the peasant farmer had left me with a powerful urge for release. "Tell me quickly, McGregor, what was said."

"My Lord, the ambassador's name is William and he has come to demand from your father twenty knights and sixty com-mon foot soldiers for his campaign against Somerset. Of course your father has little choice but to obey. William was told to rest the night and that arrangements would be made to deliver the troops in two days. The Knight has gone to the East tower to bed the night. He is a fine looking man."

"Damn you for your impudence. Now leave me." McGregor, now with a broad grin, ran off at a trot as I made my way along the dimly lit Castle corridors to the East tower. With my heart nearly pounding through my chest I knocked on the heavy oaken door. "Sir William, it is Clarence of Dunwich. I pray a word with you." I spoke softly as the object of my longing cautiously opened the portal.

"Come in, please." His voice was rich, sounding like a forest waterfall. In the firelight, his hair shimmered with sparkling highlights, his eyes twinkled like fireflies and his body stood out in silhouette like some young god of the forest. He was wearing naught but a fine white linen nightshirt, which came down just a few inches above his knees. His lightly fur-dusted shins and calf muscles and perfectly formed feet distracted me for a moment as my gaze took in their loveliness.

"I am sorry I was not able to welcome you properly to our family's Castle. I was hunting in the fields with my falcon that kept me longer then I had planned." I knew not if he knew I was not welcome in the council chamber but it was of little import. "I only wished to make sure that you were well taken care of for the night." Lord, how I longed to touch him, to remove his nightshirt, to see him in his naked splendor. My knees positively shook with desire.

"How thoughtful, Clarence. Won't you sit awhile and join me in some wine?" Within a moment I was seated on a bench near the fireplace watching him pour wine into two pewter goblets. As he handed one to me, our fingers briefly touched, sending a bolt of lightning through my hand, up my arm and straight into my heart. Our eyes locked for a second, long enough for me to know that he desired me as well for a bedmate. Knocking the goblets to the floor, I reached up and with both hands pulled William's head toward mine. Our lips parted as I thrust my tongue deep into his open throat.

I stood and locked him in my embrace. Our chests pressed together like wrestlers engaged in battle. Feeling no resistance

I backed the Knight across the room and into the bed, bending him back as my hands grabbed the fabric of his shirt and with perfect ease, ripped the cloth apart revealing the most perfectly formed chest of a man that I had ever beheld. Was anything in nature more perfect then the finely chiseled chest of man? The powerful muscles punctuated with perfectly formed tits, the flat gut with its narrow trail of light auburn hair tracing its way down to the groin, there to mingle with the thick forest of hair crowning a cock of perfect size, gently curved like a Saracen scimitar, that began already to engorge with blood, defending like a lance the two precious orbs nestled so tightly in their pouch.

In but a moment more, I was undressed myself and lay on top of my god. My hands and mouth explored every inch of his magnificent form, my own manhood stood straight at attention. We pressed wildly and rubbed voraciously together, our sweat mingling, our hearts beating like elk on the run. With my passion growing like some delicious fever I flipped the Knight onto his belly and with both hands pushed his legs apart. Then with one hand I reached around his chest, the other hand around his belly, I pulled him onto my waiting rod, thrust deep inside his ass. The sensation was like nothing I had ever known before. This powerful, celestial-like creature was mine, impaled on my manhood. My right hand found its way between his legs, there to discover his rigid pole, which dripped in anticipation of that great moment of heavenly release. But a few thrusts of my hips and the barest pressure on his cock and we both brought forth a torrent of man's milk. I fell then hard on his back, exhausted.

"We are probably damned, Clarence," he whispered through his labored breaths.

"Perhaps, but worth hellfire," I responded.

That night we lay entwined in each other's arms, our hearts gushed forth with a thousand memories: of his apprenticeship to the King's court in London, of my lonely childhood as the unwanted son of a despot, till at last we fell into an uninterrupted sleep. I awoke shortly before dawn. I watched William's chest rise and fall in gentle rhythm, my manhood once again growing to attention. What was this feeling I had for this man? Where was the bloodlust I usually felt, the need to inflict torment? It all seemed to melt away with each breath of air that escaped his gently parted lips. No, I silently berated myself. He could be the instrument of my liberation. I could totally win him over; enlist his aid in gaining the Castle for myself. Then the two of us could live together, brandishing our shared power over the vassals and Castle guards, spending countless hours together in bliss or exercising in the Castle's dungeon. The question was how to snare him into my plot. William, from what I knew so far, was an honest and kind man, a very rare trait in these dark days of plague and countless brutalities. I must make him see what a tyrant ruled this land, how our act of patricide would be for the greater good. Yes, that was the tactic. I knew that in a few hours he would be summoned back to the council chamber, and then dismissed, sent back to the King. I must act fast.

Quietly, I crept from his chamber and straightway sought out McGregor. The two of us, in the quiet of my room, prepared a list of grievances. We recounted a myriad of brutalities perpetrated against the poor downtrodden peasants, starving widows, dieing children. My list of complaints was exhaustive. I begged William to help in a quest to bring justice to Dunwich. I entreated him to give the utmost weight to this epistle and, if he agreed to assist, to let McGregor know by sending him a sprig of holly. A rather romantic idea, I thought. I did not want to sign the document lest it land into the wrong hands or that William was not the man I thought he was. Then I sealed the envelope with wax and entrusted it to McGregor's hands. He was to slip it secretly into William's saddlebag moments before his departure. From my turret window, I spied McGregor, that loathsome toad, rather than doing as he was bidden, handing the letter directly to William in full sight of my father and the Castle guard. After delivering the damning paper, I watched him retreat behind the Castle's stable. I would deal with him later. He would wish for the comfort of death before I was finished. I stood aghast watching the scene unfold below. My father tore open the missive, read a few lines, then shouted for his guards to arrest the Knight, William, who, in total confusion, dismounted and, surrounded by halberd-toting guards, was marched away back into the Castle's maw. The tyrant, for no other word seemed to fit, finished reading the letter, then turned and followed the prisoner. I could only imagine the hell that my dear William would have to endure for my overzealous behavior and damnably misplaced trust in McGregor.

My mind spun into a frenzy of rage fed by warring urges: to do everything in my power to save myself and William or to hide myself in one of the dark recesses of the dungeon and delight in the sights and sounds of what I knew would be a protracted ordeal of unimaginable pain and horror for my handsome Knight. I knew he had no idea who sent the letter, though I imagined he could well surmise its author. Would he scream out my name just to alleviate the agony of torture or hold his tongue for my sake? The more I considered my options, the stronger my urge to watch and listen. Would another man sacrifice his body for my sake? What greater proof of love then to take the rack and burning irons for the cause of another man's life? I must follow this to the end, I said in a whisper for no other ears but mine own.

I knew every secret hiding place in the Castle's dungeon, having started my observations of interrogation and punishment at an early age. I had often made myself invisible by climbing up into one of the side vaulted arches. The darkness and thick wooden beams provided shelter while affording me a panoramic view of the entire chamber. But I had to act quickly before the guards and questioners arrived with their prisoner. I knew that my father never attended these sessions, preferring to loll his time with wenches or drink.

I was safely hidden away in my ceiling perch but a few minutes when the sound of marching guards and the mumbled voices of the interrogators sent shivers of dread and yet eager anticipation through my gut.

"William Preston, in this chamber you will either confess your conspiracy and reveal the names of your fellow plotters or suffer the torments of the damned. Which shall it be?" intoned Godfrey. Henry Godfrey was an old wizened toady who took delight in his work, not so much from the thrill of inflicting agony as in achieving results, a grey functionary devoid of humor.

"I have told the Lord of the Castle that I have no idea who wrote that letter. I am on the King's business, who, when he learns of my unlawful imprisonment, will be outraged and will punish any and all those who dare lay a hand on his emissary." William said these words in a calm and deep voice, only to make me long for him the more. He held his head high, his chest puffed out standing with the strength of a god.

"Very well, we must begin. Guards, strip him and place him on the rack."

My eyes nearly bugged out of their sockets as I stared, transfixed, at the preparations. It took three over-muscled brutish guards to subdue William and rend his tunic, undergarments and boots from his body. He fought with all of his might, but in the end was felled by a few powerful knee jerks to his groin, coupled with two powerful fist jabs to his gut. Doubled over in pain and on the verge of vomiting, the now naked fellow was dragged across the rough stone floor towards the blood- and sweat-stained oaken rack. I nearly gasped at the sight of his back and leg muscles as they strained against his captors, but then, as he was forced onto his back and placed on the wooden slats, the sight of his magnificent chest, flat belly and alluring manhood sent waves of unholy pleasure up and down my spine. I felt my own rod begin to stiffen as my balls roiled in their sack. And yet what kind of monster was I that I could bear to watch the awful ordeal that was to be visited on one I presumably loved? A mystery that I had little time to ponder as I was riveted by the guards' next move, which was the tying of William's wrists to the thick rough hemp ropes that were wound around the rack's drum. I could see every drop of cold sweat that covered his chest, matting his hair close to his body and pooling down along the sides of his naked form, that soft bronzed flesh that covered his sculpted muscles, in high relief against the nearly blackened roughhewn timbers. Next his ankles were placed in stocks. I watched his perfectly formed ankles as they chafed against the wooden stocks. His bare feet seemed so sadly vulnerable in their naked confinement. William's breathing was labored as he tried to take deep breaths, perhaps in order to calm himself and gather his strength for the trials that lay ahead. His eyes darted around the room, searching out each guard's face, but at last fixing on the cold grey stare of Godfrey.

"Begin," Godfrey ominously intoned as Bruno, the guard assigned to the turning of the drum, positioned himself by the crank. A few quick revolutions of the drum and the ropes dug into William's powerful wrists; a few more turns and his arms began to raise high over his head. I could see the taut muscles and sinews begin to strain, the shoulders begin to elongate, the muscles of his chest begin to lose their sculpted half-moon curve under his tits, to stretch ever more tightly into flat plains.

"Keep turning," Godfrey instructed.

My gaze soon fell to William's face. His jaw was still firm and resolute, though I could detect the pain he must be feeling as his eyes began to wince and beads of sweat formed on his Olympian brow.

The stretching of his abdominal muscles was starting to make his breathing more difficult as he tried to keep air in his lungs as long as possible. His feet twisted wildly, trying to relieve the pressure of the wood as it bit into his ankles.

"William Preston, the rack will keep on turning till your elbows pop from their sockets, till your shoulders separate, your hips separate, and your very spine break in two or till you are no longer able to take a life-giving breath. What shall it be?" Godfrey whispered these words in William's ear as he motioned for Bruno to keep up the turning.

"I know not of this letter or its import and you will be damned by the King when he learns of this," William haltingly gasped through clenched teeth.

"Turn again, Bruno," commanded Godfrey. Ever the functionary, the dull grey man gave his orders in a monotone voice that gave striking contrast to the ghastly business at hand. Bruno put his back into the work, the drum now being much harder to turn as William's bone, sinew and muscle fought against the onslaught. The Knight's face resembled that of some poor damned soul plunging headlong into the mouth of hell. From my vantage point I could see how the tears begin to form in the corners of those dear eyes. His teeth were so locked together that it was a wonder that they did not break. With all of his will he tried not to scream. And still the relentless Bruno, with ever increasing effort, forced the drum to turn another inch, an inch that caused another tidal wave of pain. Godfrey stood close to William's head, leaning in so as not to lose a word should the prisoner say "Hold," and give over the needed information.

"Sir Godfrey, I fear that if we continue, the prisoner will pass out or that his spine will break."

"You could be right. Let us not take a chance. Bruno, lock the drum in place and bring me a scourge. Perhaps the braided whip, well applied, will loosen his tongue. Better bring some water to revive him. He looks close to exhaustion."

A bucket of cold water to awaken some poor wretch from merciful oblivion was always at the ready in the torture chamber. Godfrey stood back as Bruno dumped the icy bath onto William's head. The shock caused his eyes to open and his mouth to unbolt as he gulped for air and coughed out water splashing down his throat and into his lungs. All this caused yet more excruciating pain, as even the slightest bodily movement was like splintered glass imbedded in his muscles. His wrists and ankles, now chaffed raw from the rough hewn wood and caustic hemp, were aflame as he tried vainly to move as little as possible. His fingers and toes tensed like the claws of my dear falcon. His fine brow was a mass of wrinkled agony and the tears flowed down his cheeks like spring rain.

"William, why do you persist in this folly? You must see that we are stronger than you. But a name and this will all stop. You may, with God's good grace, be pardoned by the King. Come now, my boy. Who wrote the letter of complaint? Who are your fellow conspirators?"

And still William kept silent.

"You are in the very bloom of youth, a man with the entire world before him and such beauty of form." I had no idea Godfrey recognized beauty. Perhaps the old geezer was more human then I thought. And so he went on, "Don't make us go further, William."

"On my allegiance to the King, on my very soul, I do not know who wrote that letter. Why don't you question that scribe who handed it to me?"

"Oh fear not, that we will, once he is found, but you are here and it is to you we put the question."

"Do what you will, I will not perjure myself."

"Very well, it is your decision. Hand me the scourge, Bruno, and stand well back." The scourge was made of braided rawhide with bits of iron chips imbedded in each of the nine tips. I watched in awed silence as the old man took a position some three feet away from the outstretched naked body before him, and then saw the flash of arm and leather in the air as it sliced through the chamber, landing foursquare across William's chest. In an instant, nine red streaks punctuated by small drops of blood appeared. One red line crossing his right tit caused the helpless fellow to bellow out a curse, which was cut short by the application of a second and third strike. At each blow, Godfrey appeared to come more and more to life; invigorated by his job, he displayed a strength I would have thought long lost. And as the scourge struck again and again, William's chest soon turned crimson, the color of a Cardinal's cloak. The scourge caused special damage to his man tits, lacerating and bruising them beyond all recognition. Tiny rivulets of his precious blood wended their way down across his naked body, splattering onto the rack's thirsty surface. William tossed his head back and forth at each successive lashing, as though he were unable to comprehend the intensity of the pain. And as though that were not enough, the torturer began to take aim at his tight belly, leaving fresh lacerations at each blow. And as the whip progressed further southward, a strand of leather and iron chip or two began to glance against his manhood. This new sensation brought forth a further cry of agony. Godfrey, with the slightest of grins, then began to rain blow after blow at William's groin, turning his cock and balls into a mass of torn throbbing flesh, and still William would not break. This must be some miracle of endurance for surely no man could withstand such brutal treatment, and perhaps all for my sake he held silent. Could it be? I had little time to wonder as Godfrey, now exhausted, let the whip drop from his fist.

"Bruno, this fellow must be mad. I am exhausted. Let me sit awhile while you heat up the irons."

My God, I thought, he is to be branded. This, the torturer's ultimate weapon, almost always broke the prisoner or, after sufficient pressing on of the glowing iron, caused the victim to succumb from a surfeit of agony.

"Also bring me a short length of cord." Before I could fully fathom this request, I watched in horrified delight as Godfrey's wrinkled liver-spotted old claw grabbed William's now swollen bloody ball sack and cock and with a few perfect loops tied his manhood off into a grotesque package of engorged meat. I knew in an instant that the hot irons would be ground into his groin. William's eyes nearly popped from his head as he knew quickly what the next stage of his torment was to be. His head twisted violently back and forth. I half feared and yet hoped he would knock himself out before the moment came. Godfrey took one of the long glowing pokers from out the burning coal bucket and held if close for William to see. I could tell that the poor fellow could feel the heat as it radiated from the blazing iron.

"Beware, William; none can bear these glowing irons for long. Save yourself and give over to our demands. Who wrote the letter?"

"Die though I must, I know not and will not lie; better to succumb here then to face judgment with false witness," William screamed.

"Then suffer," Godfrey said rather dryly as be took the poker and placed the point of the iron on what was left of the fellow's right tit. The sound of sizzling flesh, a short burst of steam, burning chest hair and flesh was quickly followed by a wail of unimaginable anguish.

"Speak, or I burn the other."

"Never, be damned," William shouted with what was left of his strength. Again Godfrey placed the gleaming iron against the man's left tit. Sizzle, steam, sparks and another heart-wrenching scream followed.

"Bruno, bring more water."

William, about to pass out again, was quickly revived yet again, all in time for the next and what would prove the final onslaught.

A fresh poker was removed from the glowing embers. Godfrey raised it up for William to see, and then slowly aimed for the tied cock and balls. With perfect aim, Godfrey placed the sharp point of the rod squarely between the two tied orbs and ground the poker into the precious flesh. The scream that followed was the most ungodly sound I have ever heard and one that still lingers in my brain after all these many years. A series of long extended "No's" gushed forth from the prisoner's bloodstained lips. He futilely banged his head against the rack, trying desperately to knock himself into oblivion, but the repositioning of the iron on the sack and along the shaft of his cock only brought forth more screams of unimaginable shrillness. And I, nearly suspended from the ceiling, watched with all the horror and all the delight that a soul at war with itself could endure. My own cock throbbed to the point of bursting. It was all I could do to keep my hands from caressing my rod till climax, but fear of being seen kept me in check.

At last the screams died away and William was still. I watched as Bruno went for yet more water to be thrown onto his naked body in a vain attempt to revive him, but William's heart had failed and now he was released from this filthy world. He had died in unfathomable agony and all for me. I watched silently as

Godfrey called the hall guards to remove the lifeless body. I saw Godfrey and his men leave the chamber as they carried William's body, naked and limp, out where I presumed it would be impaled on the Castle's wall for all to see.

Well, Abbot Thomas, to finish my confession, I waited some few moments before descending from my perch, made my way from out the Castle walls and sought sanctuary here at the monastery. I left McGregor to his fate. Over the years I have oft wondered what became of him. I'm an old man now and have tried to scourge myself against impure thoughts and deeds, devoting my life to contemplation and the occasional good work, but still, in the darkness of my cell, my soul fights endless battles. Pray for me.

Your humble servant,
Clarence of Dunwich

Tank Books

The Stockade
Introduction

Blazing white heat momentarily blinded Captain Gordon as he limped off the porch steps and headed to the guard house where the three Yankee spies were being held. The captain's thin pinched lips curled ever so slightly upward in a poor excuse for a smile in anticipation of the interrogations that were about to commence. He thrived on these moments when he could exact revenge on these Yankee bastards for the loss of his right leg, the destruction of his glorious plantation and the utter ruin of his hopes for a generalship. Gordon stood nearly six feet tall with a powerful build, arms and shoulders of a field hand, the barrel chest of first class wrestler and a once handsome face that inspired both respect and desire, twisted now in a constant grimace of rage.

Spies provided the best release as they were exempt from any consideration afforded other prisoners of war and Confederate ideas of chivalry. As he made his way across the dust red compound memories of the last Yank spy that fell before him sent a wave of warm pleasure into his groin. The New England farmer, a strapping and handsome lad of twenty perhaps had lasted nearly three days under relentless torture. Flogging, branding, stretching, nothing seemed to break his stubborn will. When at last the prisoner was led to the gallows, stripped to the waist, covered in agonizing welts from the lash, chest dappled in angry bruises and tits bleeding from abuse did he falter for a moment, almost ready to give up the information Captain Gordon seemed so desperate for but then after a deep breath he thrust out is chin and mounted the steps of the scaffold as bravely as any man could wish facing the infinite. The Captain watched this proud young man while barely being able to disguise the iron like hardness of his cock that bulged inside his uniform. Yes, this was a fond memory and now he had three more prisoners to put to the question. What ever they had to say was of little concern. In this camp Gordon was judge and jury. The only thing that brought him relief from his own suffering was to relish the screams and cries of men in torment.

Part One

Sgt. Tobias of the New Hampshire 36th leaned against the jagged stone wall of the guard house gazing sadly at Corporals Peter and Mathew who were lying on the rancid straw covered floor groaning softly from the merciless beating they had endured by the ferocious Rebels not two hours ago. Ambushed some five miles outside of the tiny town of Webster, Georgia by a squad of drunken, illiterate thugs, a sorry excuse for soldiers, they were thrashed to within an inch of their lives. Then their hands were tied behind their backs and a rope around their necks they were force marched with rifles at their backs to Gordon's stockade then dumped into a holding cell.

"You boys get some rest now, ya'll hear? Captain Gordon gonna come on out here and ask you fellas some questions pretty soon," were the last words spoken by one of the Rebels before the iron bars were slammed shut and the door banged closed, leaving the three men to sweat and fear.

Tobias, a burly man of Scots-Irish decent was a rugged forty with a full beard speckled with gray and trimmed in style of his hero, the renowned General Grant. He had spent his life soldiering and had built up his body to withstand the most intense rigors of army life. His powerful thighs and calf muscles could endure countless miles of forced march with a heavy pack. His strength and stamina was always an inspiration to his men who loved him despite his caustic and bullying manner on the field of battle. Around a camp fire or when he held a dieing soldier in his arms, the Sgt. was a man of compassion worthy of a Whitman poem.

Peter and Mathew were new enlistees. They had been insep-arable as youngsters and when the war came, they joined up together swearing to stay and fight side by side to the end.

Peter was the taller of the two boys. Work on his parent's dairy farm had left him lean and strong. His blond hair, robin's egg blue eyes fair and smooth complexion, all signs of his German heritage were lusted after by every pretty girl in the county but Peter was indifferent to all their advances, preferring to spend his few hours of leisure a week with his pal. Mathew, son of a blacksmith was short but with the power of his smithy ancestor, Vulcan. Like a Greek sculpture his shoulders, arms and chest glistened with man sweat as he toiled bare-chested over the glowing fires swinging his heavy mallets. Half Irish, half Portuguese he combined the best features of both worlds; coal black hair, olive complexion and deep green eyes. His arms were covered with a soft down of curly black hair which also matted his chiseled chest and rock hard abdomen. His nipples were nearly concealed in the dense forest of hair. He was quick of temper and even quicker to use his fists, but with his mate Peter he was gentle as a Pascal lamb.

The two friends volunteered without hesitation when their Sgt. asked for men willing to infiltrate behind the lines, scout out the ammunition dump and set it ablaze.

Part Two

"You boys gotta stop that moanin' now. We got to show these Johnny Rebs what New Hampshire men are made of, no matter what they do," the Sgt. admonished as he kneeled down by Peter's head to examine his swollen eye. "Come on son, the squad will soon know we are missing, get us all out of this hell hole real soon."

Peter took at deep breath and winced at the Sgt.'s touch.

"I know Sergeant, I know, it's just mighty hard. Mathew and me, we'll show 'em, don't worry, we'll make you proud." Peter turned towards his friend Mathew and whispered,

"You alright Mathew?"

"Yup, guess so, mighty ach in my balls where that fat Reb. done kicked me but I'll be swell pretty soon."

"Sgt., what do you think they will do to us? Think they'll hang us?"

"Pete boy, I don't rightly know but I doubt it. First they'll want to know what we were doin' around here and then probably want to know where the squad is bivouacked. Remember boys, no matter what these Reb's dish out, we gotta keep our mouths shut. The lives of the entire squad and a lot more men then that are at stake. Quiet now, I hear someone comin'."

Mathew and Peter with aching limbs slowly rose to their feet ready to face whatever torments were to come.

"That's right boys, face 'em square and true."

Peter and Mathew turned their head to face each other. Both had a strong desire to grab each other's hand but the moment was lost as the rickety door to the guard house flew open with a resounding crash. An inferno of dry hot air and blinding light hit the three Yanks with the force of a tidal wave but they held their ground. In the doorway, silhouetted in the sun light was the looming shadow of Capt. Gordon, flanked by whip and rope bearing soldiers.

"I hope my men made you comfortable, always happy to welcome guests from the great state of, now where you boys from?" Capt. Gordon's unctuous manner oozed like rancid oil.

"Come on boys, no harm in telling us where you hale from, now is there?"

"We are New Hampshire men," Sgt. Tobias said with all the pride a citizen of the Granite State could muster. "And we got separated from our squad. We trust that we will be treated honorably like prisoners of war just like we treat Confederate soldiers."

Capt. Gordon gave a wan smile, nodded his head ever so slightly then turned to the two guards, "Open the cell, bring the two young ones out into the yard, and leave the Sgt. here for awhile." Gordon gave the command which was rapidly obeyed, accomplished with much pushing, yanking and a few good fist blows to Mathew and Peter's already sore guts and aching groins. Doubled up in pain the two Corporals were easily dragged from the cell and out into the yard as Sgt. Tobias with a rifle pointed at his head stood helplessly by.

"Be brave boys, be brave, you'll be alright boys." The Sgt. kept repeating, hoping against hope that these lads would somehow survive.

"We will Sgt., we will." Peter and Mathew said in tandem, fighting the growing lumps in their throats that belied their bravery.

Tank Books

Part Three

The blinding white glare of the high noon sun and the swelter-ing heat of a Georgia July day hit the two captives like the kick of a mule. In their already weak and terrified condition, their knees began to buckle but for the vice-like grip of their escort they surely would have sunk to the ground.

Captain Gordon followed the grim parade and shouted, "Strip them to the waist and tie them to the whipping posts."

Mathew and Peter, with heads held high but with feet drag-ging in the dust were quickly lead to two sweat and blood stained pine posts planted firmly in the ground each of which had an iron ring embedded some seven feet from the base. Two teams of Rebs worked with practiced efficiency, one man shredding the Yanks shirts and under ware, the other deftly grabbing and tying wrists together with a rope long enough to thread through the iron ring. Once the captives were stripped the ropes were yanked up forcing the boys arms up agonizingly over their head, their backs pressed painfully against the splinters of the post. A stream of sweat ran down each of their chests. Mathew's hairy chest became matted with perspiration: a thin trickle formed ,meeting the fine line of hair that ran like an arrow from the base of his sternum down his belly and disappearing into the waist of his trousers. Peter's pale white skin glistened like highly pol-ished marble. His perfectly round tits, pulled now to ovals by the extreme pressure of the rope each held a single drop of moisture making them glisten like pale pink diamonds, a sight that did not go unnoticed by Capt. Gordon. Their chests rose and fell with their labored breathing as they tried to regain some sense of bravery and to brace themselves for what torments were to come.

"We'll leave these two here for a spell to enjoy our Georgia sun, enjoy the company of our notorious horse flies and think about what they have to tell us.

I'll be back gentlemen after a cool drink and an afternoon rest." Captain Gordon turned towards his rooms, dismissed the sentry guards and disappeared into the cool shade of his porch.

"Mathew, Mathew, are you alright? Damn these Rebs, what do you think, think the squad will get here in time to save our necks?" whispered Peter through already parched lips. His eyes were shut against the acid like stinging of the sweat that poured down from his forehead into his eyeballs.

"I don't know." croaked Mathew, "Better not talk to much, waste a'time anyways."

"I know, but I sure didn't want to die like this friend, sure as shootin', I didn't want to die like this."

"Hush now."

The two Yanks let their heads droop forward and tried to rest, the heat acting like a narcotic slowing down the rhythm of their breathing and beat of their stout young hearts.

But only a few minutes past before the buzzing of several hungry horse flies began to circle their heads. Then needle like pincers began seeking nourishment in the firm young flesh strung up so tantalizingly before the flies. Mathew and Peter's eyes, almost at the same time snapped open as the flies began to bite into their chests, their foreheads, their bellies, their backs. The two men tried to wriggle about to keep the flies from biting but the ropes only grew tighter, the bound bodies even better targets. And so the flies continued to swoop and rend drawing tiny drops of blood that mingled with their sweat.

Captain Gordon, sitting on his rocking chair smiled as he watched the two handsome youths gyrate, their chests and legs undulating in an almost erotic dance of pain.

"Bring more rope, and tie them tighter to the poles." Gordon shouted to one of the guards half dozing in the shade nearby.

The Reb. aroused himself, went to the supply room and brought out two more lengths of rope which he expertly used to tie Peter and Mathew. He wound the rope around their chests, the rough hemp digging savagely into their flesh, positioned just below their tits.

Then the rope was secured tightly around their bellies and tied in unrelenting knots behind the post. Unable now to move more then an a quarter of an inch at best, the two were totally at the mercy of the unrelenting flies drawn now in greater number by the sent of man sweat and blood.

"God save us." screamed Mathew trying to bang his head into the pole, hoping to knock himself out.

"I'm going crazy, damn to hell these flies of Satan." screeched Peter, likewise knocking his head against the poles."

"Bind their heads, don't want them to hurt them selves," chuckled Capt. Gordon.

The order was quickly obeyed as the flies swarmed in ever increasing numbers. The swooped and dived into the tightly bound heads, necks, chests, bellies and backs of the two screaming Yankee captives.

Their voices grew louder and louder in high pitched agony till at last their throats and tongues were to dry to resonate their pain.

And Gordon rocked and rocked, his right hand slowly moving from his thigh to rest ever so lightly on his crotch, his manhood starting to engorge as he listened, watched, and waited for the sun to set.

Part Four

Tobias paced the tiny cell like a caged wild beast. He would roar with all his might from rage but mostly in an attempt to blot out the screams.

"You God forsaken heathen, you damned sons of bitches, what are you doing to them?" He shouted mightily with only the air to listen. "If I get out of here I will kill you all with my bare hands, make you scream like women. You son's of bitches." And then the good Sgt. would shake the unyielding iron bars. Exhausted at last he slumped down on the floor, covered his ears with his hands and wept. He doubted if the Yank squad, already badly depleted from numerous squrmiches with Johnny Reb would risk an attempt at rescue. Damn it to hell, he had to find a way to save these two brave young lads.

"Bring me a bottle of whiskey, got a mighty thirst watchin' these two fellas."

"Yes, Captain Gordon."

Mathew and Peter were now near to the breaking point. Their faces, chests, arm pits, bellies and back were stippled with countless bites and the flies continued to bite into their half naked and defenseless bodies.

Gordon new that if their hearts gave out or they went out of their heads the entertainment would end plus they may actually have some information worth having about troop movements or their mission.

"You corporal, bring a bucket of water when you bring that whiskey."

"Yes sir."

Corporal Collins ran into the Capt.'s quarters for the whiskey, all the time shaking his head. He knew this wasn't right, not right at all treatin' these young fellas this way. Oughtta be something he could do for 'em, poor wretches, even if they were damn dirty Yankees. Nope, just wasn't right.

On the far side of the yard, behind a high wire fence more then a dozen bedraggled Yankee prisoners stood watching the pathetic sight. Most of them were too sick or beaten down to make much of a stir though several huddled together making plans. Maybe there was some way to help these two unfortu-nates.

Guards stood guard around the perimeter of the yard, on top of towers while others rested in what limited shade the stockade provided, cleaning rifles or just dozing. Most of the Rebels were used to Captain Gordon's idea of sport. They had seen him work over more then one captured Yankee. Didn't matter much any-way, what's one or two more sufferin' Yanks.

"Your whiskey, Sir."

"'Bout time soldier. Now leave that bucket a'water beside me here."

"Yes Sir, Capt. Gordon." "Bastard" the Corporal whispered to himself.

Gordon took a nice long swig from his bottle, smacked his lips then slowly rose up using his knurled walking stick for leverage, leaned down and picked up the bucket of water and slowly made his way across the yard to the whipping posts. The captives were nearly unconscious. He studied each in turn. "Such handsome young men. I was once comely myself, had no end of young studs longing to get into my pants, a few women too. Now look at me. I'm gonna make these Yanks pay dearly for what they did to me. Break 'em, that's what I'm gonna do, real slow, break 'em so they just beg me to put 'em out of their misery."

The splash of the water thrown against the two lads drove the flies into the air and off to the stables where they would vex some poor horses. Mathew and Peter slowly began to revive. Their eyes began to flutter open as they tried to get their bearings. Though each longed to look at the other the tight ropes around their forehead prevented any lateral movement.

"You boys like our Georgia flies. Recon they's the biggest in the south, and bite, Lordy, can they bite, but I guess you two know that now, don't ya?"

"Now listen here you damn Yankees, I got some questions for you and you better answer straight or its off to the gallows, but not before you have a chance to experience a little more of our southern hospitality. Now, I want to know what you and that broken down Sgt. locked up over yonder were up to, hiddin' out in that farm house. Then you gotta tell me where you squad's bivouacked at. You hear me lads?"

Peter was the first to answer, "Captain, we told you and your men we got separated a few days ago from our outfit. We was just tryin' to get a bit of shut eye and maybe snag a chicken for some food."

Captain Gordon moved directly in front of Peter, glared at him long and cold in the eyes then with one swift movement like a cobra drove his fist into the captive's groin where his fingers circled the helpless nut sack through the well worn fabric of his uniform trousers. He smiled then grabbed and yanked down with all his might.

Peter let out a wale of pain, his eyes bulging in his head from the agony and the suddenness of the onslaught.

"Now you don't think I'm a stupid Southern cracker do you boy?"

"Let him go you bastard." Mathew managed to croak through swollen lips and parched tongue.

"You two are in for a lot more then a little nut grabbin', just you wait. Corporal Collins, get some men over here. Strip these fells down to their birthday suits and be quick."

Part Five

"Captain Gordon Sir, a message from headquarters." Lance Corporal Williams shouted breathlessly as he ran across the yard waving a letter that had just been delivered.

"Give it here." Gordon snapped, "Now get these two fells stripped down while I read this here message."

Two of the more brutish stockade guards, Wallace and Jeb, were only too happy to oblige. In a matter of seconds calloused hands scratched, clawed, ripped and tore away Mathew and Peter's trousers and their pathetically worn under ware. With some degree of struggle their mud stained boots were yanked from their blistered feet. A pile of torn uniforms and broken down boots lay on the ground gathering dust.

"Hoo wee, lookey here at these two Yanks, they's sure are hung."

"Lordey you said a mouth full."

Peter and Mathew turned crimson with humiliation. Both young men were indeed well endowed, a constant source of friendly amusement in the barracks. Peter's cock was long and slender and crowned with a thin wisp of blond hair. His balls hung low and were likewise peppered with a soft down of light blond hair. Mathew on the other hand, while not blessed with great length sported a thick cock with a considerably large bulbous head. His pubic hair was a forest of thick black. His balls were tight up against his groin but were nevertheless prodigious in size.

"You two, cut 'em down and put 'em back in their cell, we got company comin'.

Need to save 'em up for tonight when General Whitely gets here. He enjoys a good interrogation." Gordon gave the command, gave a parting glance to the two captives, giving an especially long glance at their male members, crumpled the message into his pocket and hobbled off to his office.

"You two got a little reprieve but Lord help you two. I heard stories of General Whitely and you think our Captain Gordon is a mean one, just you two fells wait till the General gets a hold of ya." The two guards bantered on as they untied the two men who nearly collapsed to the ground as the ropes were loosened.

"Get a move on Yanks." One of the guards bellowed giving first Mathew then Peter a good hard kick in the buttocks which propelled them on across the dust bowl of a yard back to their prison cell. Each time the two hapless captives collapsed face forward from exhaustion they were met with a rain of kicks to their backsides.

At long last after many a fall and start they landed in a heap in the cell. Sgt. Tobias was livid with rage at the sight of his two comrades.

"You dirty, stinkin', no account good for nothins. The devil take you all." He shouted as he quickly kneeled down to get a better look at his two men.

"Careful there Sgt. they way you talk, you gonna get yours tonight along with these two fellas. Rest up boys." The two guards were nearly doubled over with laughter as they left the three to while away the hours till the Generals arrival.

"Lord save us, Mathew, Peter." The Sgt. didn't know which man to help first.

Part Six

"Welcome General."

Captain Gordon saluted his superior and ushered him into his cramped but tidy office.

"Have a seat General. Would you care for a little refreshment Sir? I have a bottle of fine Kentucky sour mash."

General Whitely nodded with much enthusiasm. His bulbous veined noise, slightly bloated face and yellow eyes bespoke his passion for the bottle. The two things he enjoyed the most in this world of tears was a good stiff drink and war. He thrived on the sights and sound of men in combat. The struggling, screaming bleeding sight of men in torment gasping in anguish either on the field or in the prison stockade where his great joy. He knew he should be ashamed of the erotic thrill it gave him but damn it all, he didn't care a jot for all these moral scruples. Men were made strong and powerful to suffer. That was their beauty and if he enjoyed the sight as much as some men enjoyed a beautiful woman, so be it!

In Captain Gordon he had found a fellow enthusiast and whenever possible made a point of including Gordon's stockade on his inspection tours.

"Thank you Gordon, I believe I will and make it a stiff one. Been ridin' all day in this heat, have a mighty thirst."

"Here you are General." Gordon said as he poured out an equal measure for himself and took a seat behind his desk.

"The General has come at a most auspicious time. We have captured three Yankee spies. Two young recruits and a staff Sgt. Sort of a mother hen the Sgt. is but mighty big and power-ful, the other aren't uncomely either. All in good shape they are, should provide quite an evening's entertainment while we question them."

"Well done Gordon. Nothing would give me greater pleasure. Where are they now?"

"In the guard house restin' up from the afternoon."

"You have a couple of stout fellows that can help us? Don't want any bleedin' heart soldiers if you know what I mean? Need to find a pair of mean sons of bitches who won't get squeamish at a little blood and won't talk later."

"I have just the men General. Wallace and Jeb, two more onry mountain boys you would be hard pressed to find."

"Good, then pour me another stiff one and let's not keep our Yankee friends waitin' another minute. Might as well bring the bottle, this could be a long night, what do you say Gordon?"

"An inspired idea General. Corporal Williams, get Jeb and Wallace have them fetch the three Yankees in the guard house meet us at the tool shed. Tell 'em to bring some rope and a pair of bull whips."

"Yes, right away Captain." Williams said with just a note of pity in his voice for the poor unfortunates.

The tool shed! The name always sent a shiver down any of

the stockade's inmates; either POW or guard, for it was from this diabolical place that the screams of men being punished or interrogated often filled the night air. The tool shed was actually a decrepit horse barn. Six stalls and over head beams dark now with smoke, dust, and mold were perfect for restraining men. The straw covered floor was an ideal sop for the sweat and blood that would invariably drip from the naked bound bodies. Three sturdy chairs, a small table and coal stove were all the creature comforts the barn had to offer.

General Whitely and Gordon barely had time to pour themselves another whiskey when the barn door opened with a bang. Wallace and Jeb had tied a rope around the three prisoner's necks, tied their hands behind their backs and marched them in. Mathew and Peter were still stark naked yet despite their humiliation and exhausted bodies held their heads high and their chests thrust out as though they were headed for an inspection by Lincoln himself. Sgt. Tobias had coached them well.

"Wallace, tie the Sgt. to a chair, the other two, string them up over the beams, spread their legs and tie their ankles to the uprights. Make 'em look like wishbones from a tom turkey."

"With pleasure sir."

"Yes sir."

Wallace and Jeb were expert at the art of restraining struggling prisoners and these three were a formidable match. Not till Jeb pounded his fist into the Sgt.s' gut forcing the big man to double up in pain was he able to slam him down into a chair and rope his hands behind his back. A bit of rope around each ankle and chair leg and another length around Tobias' chest convinced the Sgt. that more struggle was useless. Meanwhile the two naked captives were quickly suspended above the floor. Their ankles were soon tied tight to uprights leaving them drawn tight. Their fine strong muscles pulled taught gleamed with sweat from the flickering candle on the table. Shadows played about the barn like some hellish dance. The barn had retained all the heat and humidity from the scorching afternoon so their bodies dripped sweat splashing noiselessly into the straw. Peter and Mathew were afraid. Afraid like they had never been before. Their eyes practically bugged out of their handsome faces as they fixed their gaze on the Sgt. beseeching him with their looks for help or some comfort. The Sgt. for his part stared back in a vain attempt to reassure his two men that they would survive. Maybe help was just moments away his eyes seem to say.

Gordon polished off another swig of whiskey and in a half drunken slur said, "Now you two boys, get those bull whips and give these Yankees a whipping, make 'em sing for us. That is, unless the Sgt. here wishes to tell us what the hell they was up to?"

"Damn you to hell Sir." Tobias shouted.

"We were hopin' you would say that Sgt. So boys, begin."

"Pass me the bottle Gordon." A now slightly drunk Whitely whispered, unable to take his eyes off the two naked, roped, stretched young men so tantalizing displayed. The General's right hand rested lightly between his legs as he raised his left hand to receive the bottle.

"Yes, a mighty pretty sight Gordon. Get to it you men, you heard your Captain's orders."

The sudden snap of two whips cut through the muggy air like the crack before thunder followed in short order by two high pitched yelps from the stretched and helpless Yankees.

Another snap, another collision of rawhide against human

flesh followed by another anguished scream that kept repeating over and over. Gordon and Whitely sat in their wooden chairs, backs straight, slowly sipping whiskey and with their free hand massaging their ever swelling cocks and roiling balls.

"Yes Gordon, you sure know how to entertain a General" Whitely mused as the whips flew in the air. After three or four lacerations, questions were put to the men only to be met with silence. The whipping ended with well over a hundred strokes. The soldiers' backs were a torrent of blisters and scolding pain but they held true.

Tank Books

Part Seven

"I think they done passed out Captain." Jeb called out as he let his whip droop to his side.

"Sure thing Captain." Confirmed Wallace.

"You bastards!" shouted Tobias as he struggled vainly in the chair.

"Cut them down but hog tie 'em so they don't think they're getting away.

"Yes Captain." Jeb and Wallace responded in unison.

"And now for you Sgt. Perhaps it is time for us to ask you a few questions. What do you say General. Let us see how much a tough Yankee Sgt. can take."

"A lovely idea Captain. What did you have in mind?"

As the Captain pondered the many delicious possibilities a large stable rat scampered across the straw and disappeared into a hole in the wall.

Gordon's lip began to adjust into the slightest of smiles as his eyes began to twinkle with delight.

"Yes, General I have an idea. You two, damn you both hurry up with those ropes then fetch me a rat and a cage."

"Why Captain Gordon, what do you have in mind?"

Tobias with eyes virtually bugging out of his head as he had a particular loathing of rats, struggled ever more violently against the rough ropes. But instead of loosening the hemp it only grew tighter digging mercilessly into his wrists and ankles.

"Ah, I see we have created some interest from our good Sgt. Another whiskey, General while we wait? And while the men are out huntin', shall we take a look at the snake the Sgt. has between his legs. Some nice morsel for our rat."

"Why Captain, what a splendid idea. Pass the bottle and let's take a look."

Tobias could hardly believe what he was hearing from these two fiends. What kind of heathens were they? In his terror he hardly noticed his two men now hog tied and lying unconscious on the filthy straw. Their backs, asses and legs crisscrossed with lacerations from the fierce bull whipping they had received.

Gordon took the bottle, downed a large swig of burning whiskey then stumbled in a drunken stupor toward the bound Sgt. Nearly falling head first into Tobias' lap he reached for the captive's trouser buttons. His fumbling fingers at last managed to undo the crotch while the Sgt. struggled violently almost knocking himself and chair over.

"Ah, here we are." Gordon mumbled as he reached into the Sgt.'s pants and grabbed for the cock and balls which with much twisting and yanking he managed to expose.

"Why Sgt. you are more like a stallion then a man. Look here General. Did you ever see so much meat between a man's legs?"

General Whitely stumbled over to take a look. What he saw took his breath away. Tobias sported a pair of enormous balls and a thick long cock which despite his fear and resistance began to engorge with blood at the rough handling. For the truth was as much as Tobias fought his nature it was for men that he truly lusted. The hand of a man on his genitals, even one that he feared and loathed had a stimulating effect.

"General, this will make a nice meal for our rat. Now where in the hell are those two, what's taken' so long?" he shouted.

Part Eight

Corporal Collins had snuck into the barn at the height of the whipping and now he and Williams were huddled together on the far side of the barn. Neither had any great love for the Northern cause and in battle were only to happy to point and fire at the Blue Coats but they both knew what was going on inside the barn was not right. They held nothing but contempt for Captain Gordon having been scapegoats during many of his drunken rages.

"Ain't right what they's doin' to those guys." Corporal Williams whispered to his friend.

"I know, but what can we do about it. Don't want to get shot for disobeyin' orders now."

"Guessin' your right. This damn war. Ya know I got an idea. General Lee's headquarters is not too far. The General sure wouldn't cotton to this kind of goins on. What if we got word to Lee somehow? Come on; let's see what we can do." As silently as possible the two corporals crept silently out of the barn, across the dark compound and disappeared into Capt. Gordon's darkened office.

"I said where the hell is that damn rat, stupid hayseeds, can't even find a little ole rat" Gordon shouted at no one in particular as the General now fully in his cups drained the last of the whiskey bottle and slumped down in his chair, half passed out but still aroused at the blurred sight of the two naked bound captives lying at his feet.

"Here we are Captain, got a nice fat one." Said Jeb as he marched into the barn holding the screaming rat by its tail. "Wallace here got a nice little wooden box to put him in.

Now what do you want us to do Captain."

"Took you two damn long enough.   Strip this Yankee then spread 'em out wide on the ground. Rope his wrists and ankles so he can't move. General, wake up General, don't want to miss the fun?" Gordon lurched into the middle of the barn to watch his two henchmen carry out his orders. "That's it boys, strip him good and naked, make the rope tight like you tien' down a bronc. He's gonna pull real hard.   Once you done that make a good size hole in the bottom of the box, then yank that Yank's pole into plain sight."

The General hearing these words forced himself to stand and watch the proceedings. This was too good to be true. Damn, this Gordon had a mean streak and he liked it, Whitely mused to himself.

Sgt. Tobias with heart pounding like a military drum, a cold sweat of fear coating his large muscular frame was dragged to the center of the barn, stripped, spread eagled with arms and legs tied to vertical posts and prepared for the coming ordeal.

"Nooooooo, for the love of God nooooooo." Tobias pleaded looking first at Gordon then the General. "What kind of monsters are you?"

"Sgt. you can stop this right here and now just tell us your mission and where the rest of your dirty Yankees is hiding and we will all have a nice friendly drink."

94

Gordon was starting to feel sick from the whiskey, the stinking heat of the barn and the excitement. He sat down where he stood, "Damn, gotta rest up for a minute, damn, head's swimming. Gotta rest." Gordon mumbled as he slid further down into the straw and quickly passed out. The General taking his cue from Gordon decided a little shut eye was not a bad idea, collapsed in his chair, head resting on the table and joined the Captain in a little shut eye.

"Damn Jeb, what should we do?" said Wallace.

"Better not start this without these two drunks awake and ready to watch. I know what excites these two. Put the rat over in the tack box, let's us go get a drink ourselves. These two will be out for a few hours. These Yanks aren't goin' anywhere, they's tied good n tight."

Jeb and Wallace glanced at their two superior offices, shook their heads then left to find a bottle of their own.

"Mathew, Peter... Mathew, Peter, wake up men, you alright, you gonna be alright." Tobias whispered as he struggled against the ropes.

Mathew was the first to open his eyes but he winced as the flood of pain from his lacerated back and his aching muscles contorted by the rope were too much to bare right away.

"Peter, hey Peter, wake up soldier, wake up." Mathew whispered to his friend.

"Those Rebs are passed out, we gotta get free, gotta get out a here before they kill us."

Said the Sgt.

But try as they all did the Rebs had done to good a job at roping. Southern farm hands knew how to make knots that would hold.

Mathew and Peter slipped in and out of consciousness exhausted by their ordeals with sun, flies and rawhide. The good Sgt., only slightly more comfortable, lay in agony not for himself but for fear of what more might happen to his two brave men. He turned his head as much as possible to gaze at their badly beaten bodies. Tears welled up in his kind Irish eyes. He loved these two lads like they were his sons. Damn these Rebs, Damn these two sick devils' spawn sons of bitches. Would help ever come or where they to end up tortured to death.

The minutes turned to hours as Gordon and Whitley snored like two drunken bums sleeping it off in the slammer. It wasn't till just before dawn that the sounds of neighing horses, the shouts of men exchanging salutes and the stomp of military boots brought the two commanders back to the world of the living.

"What the hell." Mumbled Gordon as he rubbed the sleep from eyes. "Wake up General. Something is going on in the yard. Look sharp Whitely."

The General was an even worse hangover was barely able to open his eyes before the barn door burst open flooding the gloom with morning light. Silhouetted in the door was half of General Lee's staff.

Before the sun reached high noon Gordon was in the guard house, General Whitely was relieved of duty and the three Yanks were headed to Andersonville to face the unknown.

The Wreck of the Patroclus
Part One

Mykos and Davidis were twins. It was near to impossible to distinguish them one from the other. Even their own mother had to look closely before addressing them.

Now they were grown to full manhood. They stood five feet, nine inches in their stocking feet. Both had long thick black hair, deep dark eyes framed with perfectly formed eye brows and long full lashes, full sensuous lips and dazzling white teeth. Their powerful arms, legs, and chests were perfectly toned reminding one of statues of their ancient Greek ancestors. As soon as they were old enough to sail they had joined their father's fishing boat. The years of sun, wind and hard work had built them into strapping Greek gods.

The brothers shared more then physical beauty. When they were boys their emotional bond was as strong as any iron chain in the port of Perius, the seaport that they called home. They hardly had to speak to know each others thoughts and desires.

And yet as they grew into manhood and despite their profound love for each other they began to grow apart. Davidis harbored the green monster of jealousy deep in his bosom towards his brother, for he knew that Mykos was infatuated with the sailor Kikon who worked on the freighter Patrocilus. Had the young sailor lived on Mount Olympus he would have been the envy of Apollo. Years of working as a sponge fisherman had burnished his skin a rich copper color. Lifting and hauling nets and ropes had toned his muscles that would have inspired a Praxateles sculpture.

The two had been friends since childhood and as the boys grew older they shared a desire for each others touch. On warm summer nights after the days hard work was done they would meet secretly to lie in each others arms and experience the power of love that a man can feel for another man.

Whenever Mykos and Kikon went off to the tavern, for a naked swim in their favorite cove, or for long walks in the hills about the port Davidis would sulk around the town and haunt the local bars where he would down endless glasses of ouzo. But when Mykos returned from one of his trysts, his jealous twin hid his rage and behaved as though nothing was wrong keeping his anger down like a caped volcano.

The scorching summer sun rose over the harbor as Mykos and Kikon sat on the beech making their plans.

"Kikos, what do you think your family will think about you shipping out with me?"

"I think my father will be furious since he will be short one man on his boat and Davidis will rage and get drunk. It is better for my brother and me to lead our own lives so this is a good thing only I have to convince him of that. But mostly I do not care what others think. I love you man, and want to be with you, we can explore the world together and get out of this stinking port." Mykos put his arm around his friend and drew him down into the warm sand where they embraced allowing their hands and tongues to explore each others strong lithe bodies. The young men's hearts were filled to over flowing with their passion.

Davidis had followed his brother to the sea shore and now lay on his stomach peering over the edge of the bluff gazing down at the naked scene below. His heart was filled with sadness which soon metastasized into a jealous rage. He should be there lying in Kikon's arms, not his brother. He knew as sure as the tide would turn that he would be revenged.

The following morning before first light, Mykos with small duffle bag slung over his shoulder crept from the family home and trotted like a young gazelle through the narrow cobbled streets of the ancient port to the harbor. There, waiting on the dock was his beloved friend Kikon who greeted him with open arms. The two young bucks collided into each other and turned in a whirlwind embrace, then without a word they ran down the pier and bounded up the gang plank as the ship's whistle sounded the first alert for sailing.

The early 1950's was a time of unrest around the Mediterranean coast, particularly along the shores of Libya where the freighter Patroclus was headed. There, bandits and pirates prayed on foundering vessels or thieves in leaky boats attacked unsuspecting ships at night where the villains would take the crew hostage, turning them into slaves or torturing them just for some savage bloodlust. The unlucky sailors who were unfortunate enough to fall into the hands of these pirates were often never heard of again. A few managed to escape or were ransomed by their wealthy families but most poor sailors had no such luck. It was into this cauldron of danger that the two young lovers were now sailing.

Davidis had lain awake that night and once he heard his brother depart the house, had followed at a safe distance. Now he stood on the dock as the freighter sailed south into the unknown.

Benghazi was a cesspool masquerading as a sea port. It was there that the Patroclus was bound. Her cargo of Greek wine masked the crates of Russian rifles and grenades that were destined for the war lord Ali Ben Surfit. Ali and has band of cut-throat pirates camped some ninety miles in land from the sea. They had terrorized the shipping lanes off the cost of Libya since before the Second World War. Now that the war was over and trade once more flourished they hoped to continue their thieving on the highways that lead to and from Tripoli. Ali had assembled some of the most violent blood thirsty rogues in all of North Africa. Nothing was beneath their depraved souls. Slave trading, torturing, kidnapping, stealing, it was all the same.

Ali was a giant of a man with coarse Neanderthal features, ham-fisted and powerful. He swaggered and bullied his men into blind obedience. He paid his fellow rogues well and provided them with plenty of blood sport to satiate their perverse hungers. Ali was also a man with a dream. He hoped to amass sufficient funds and arms to someday carve out his own Sheikdom. No small dreamer he.

Ali and his men had no intention of paying for their shipment of arms rather they planned to take the Patroclus before she reached port. Her crew of twelve could be easily over taken and those that survived the initial hijacking would either be killed, preferably in an entertaining fashion or brought into the desert and there sold as slaves to one of the local Emirs. And with any luck there may be a good looking young buck or two that would fetch a handsome price. Time would tell.

The night was perfectly still. High clouds obscured what would have been a full moon. The sea was like a frozen sheet of black lava brushed by a bone dry wind from the south.

The heat below deck was like an oven set for baking a roast. Mykos and Kikon, stripped to the waist climbed the ladder from their sleeping quarters and padded softly across the still frying pan hot deck. With towels in hand the made their way to the stern and lay down to catch what little breeze wafted their way. The two lovers turned on their sides to face each other.

"What do you think Benghazi is going to be like Kikon?"

"I've heard from other sailors that it is a rough port but they have great hash, handsome boys, and plenty of cheap things to by in the bazaar. Maybe you could get something to take home as a peace offering?"

"Kikon, I have no regret about leaving my home. Being here with you on the ocean like this is all that I could wish for."

"The same for me, come here." And so the two men once more despite the sultry night air embraced, their sweat soaked chests pressing close together. The other sailors on the Patroclus knew these two men were lovers and so left them alone neither condemning nor approving their love. And so the ship chugged ever further south. The old engines ratted and groaned in the night air. The lookout who was sitting on the bow of the ship smoked his pipe and drifted in and out of sleep never hearing the pirate's skiff approaching. The Patroclus anchored a few miles north of the port since she was not guaranteed a berth till the morning. This was all part of Ali's plot which so far was going just as planned. With the freighter dead in the water, the pirates were able to pull along her port side, throw their grappling hooks up over the rail and like rats scamper up the side of the ship.

The Captain was just leaving the bridge when the first shot was fired. Mykos and Kikon jumped up only to be forced to take cover behind a stanchion as bullets whizzed about their heads. The battle for the ship was short and bloody. The hands sleeping in their hammocks had no time to defend themselves. The Captain lay dead at the foot of the bridge ladder. The first mate and chief engineer were wounded and lying on the deck. Six of the hands were climbing up on to the deck followed by two of Ali's thugs holding machine guns.

"My God Kikon, what are we going to do? Shall we jump overboard and swim for it?"

"Yes, it's only a kilometer to the beach. But quiet. They will shoot us dead if they catch us. Come on."

The two lovers, sliding on their bellies made their way to edge of the deck and slowly lowered themselves into the warm water. With all the commotion on deck the pirates did not hear the two splashes as their bodies hit the sea.

Both young men were experienced swimmers but even so the distance and current made for a long slow swim. The sea had carried them north of the port so when at last they found themselves nearing a deserted inlet their excitement and joy at still being alive was almost overwhelming. At last the two, nearly drowned men made their way up onto the beech. Kikon had to give his hand to Mykos the last few steps. Then they collapsed into each others arms as small waves caressed their exhausted bodies lying on the warm sand.

Their pleasure at escaping the pirates was short lived. Two of Ali's men had been posted at this very inlet where the arms shipment was to be unloaded from the Patroclus before she was scuttled. "What do we have here? Two little fishes beached themselves."

"Get up you two. You from the Patroclus? Well my boys, you can't escape that easily."

The two pirates prodded the men in the ribs with the barrels of their machine guns and forced them to stand.

"Hands over your hands."

"Nice looking lads. Ought to fetch a good price and we should get a reward from Ali."

"Come on; get a move on you two, back up the beach. Move it!"

Mykos and Kikon looked at each other, silently communicating with each other that they had better do as they were told, at least for now.

The beech was narrow so it took only a few steps to reach the rocks where a few wind twisted cedars managed to struggle out of the ground.

"Tie these two up."

"What shall I use?"

"Idiot, go to the truck and get some chain. Move your ass. The boat should be here in a few minutes. I'll keep an eye on these two. Look like drowned rats. Don't think they will go far. You two, sit down keep your hands on top of your heads."

"What are you going to do to us?" Mykos spoke first.

"We don't have anything, my friends family are poor fishermen, my family is dead, won't get any ransom money for us. Let us go man. We won't... ahhhhhhh."

The pirate raised his rifle and slammed the butt end into Kikon's gut. He doubled over and collapsed on the ground, balling himself up like a possum. Mykos crawled to his side and pulled him close.

"I said keep your fucking hands on your head or you'll get worse."

Mykos reluctantly left his lover to writhe on the sand as he moved a few inches away and placed his hands, firmly clasped on top of his head.

The second pirate soon returned with two lengths of chain and two pad locks.

"Get up you two…move over to those trees."

In a matter of minutes Mykos and Kikon were sitting on the ground, leaning against two of the cedars with oil crusted chains wrapped tightly around their chests and wrists.

"Better gag them."

"With what? They don't have shirts."

"There is some electric tape in the back of the truck. Must I think of everything?"

Just as the dumb one was moving back to the road, a flair was seen streaking up from the black sea.

"Wait, there's Ali's signal. Come on."

From over the horizon the silhouette of the Patroculus could be seen as it was making its way full steam ahead towards the beech. Ali and his men were going to run her aground, then off load the arms and perhaps a create or two of the Greek wine.

Mykos and Kikon sat in silence, their eyes focused on their ship which would soon be torn to shreds on the rocky shallows.

"Kikon, I'm afraid."

"Hush, don't want that bastard to come back and gag us.

I'll get us out of this. It is because of me that you are in this mess."

With a groan like a stuck boar the freighter rammed into the rocks and listed to her port.

The pirates on her decks had braced themselves for the grounding. The surviving crew members were hog tied and lying on their guts on the deck.

"Come on, get a move on. Get some ropes, start getting these boxes out of the hold and lower them to the beach."

Ali, after giving his commands lowered himself into the shallow water and waded ashore.

Spying the two sailors chained to the trees he approached the two lookouts.

"What the hell do we have here? Nice work. These two must have jumped ship. Very nice. Make sure they don't get away. I will have some fun with one of them and sell the other. Keep them chained and throw them in the back of the truck after we're loaded."

Part Two

Davidis' head rested on the table, an empty shot glass and over turned bottle near by.

He had not gone to sea since his brother and Kikon had left last week, spending his time drinking and avoiding the blows and screams of his father. He felt like one half of his life was missing by the absence of his brother and the other half missing by the loss of Kikon. Tears once again streamed down his dark handsome face which was shaded with seven day's growth which only accentuated his masculine beauty.

"Damn him, damn them both." He muttered as the bar keep put his hand on his head and said, "Time to go home Davidis. Be a man. Get over this."

"Fuck you."

"Get out of my bar; don't come back till you know how to hold your liquor."

Davidis hung his head low and stumbled out into the moon lit street.

As he made his way up the dark alley towards home he heard a woman's scream come from a nearby balcony.

"The Patroclus went aground, all hands lost." These words and many more of lamentation could be heard echoing up and down the harbor district.

Davidis tried to clear his head from too much drink. He needed to think. He couldn't believe that if the freighter went aground that his brother and Kikon had been lost. He knew of the pirates and the slave trade, of the awful tortures that were inflicted on sailors unlucky enough to find themselves marooned. My God, he must do something he thought. He started to run back down the hill towards the pier. He must do something.

The pirates were quick to load their trucks. If a military patrol were to come by, their lives would not be worth a grain of sand. Once the munitions were loaded, four of the pirates herded the captive sailors into a closed van, tossing the two lovers into the mix of legs, arms and torsos all jumbled together with rope and chain like human refuse.

"Be careful with those two. Don't damage them you idiots. When we get back to camp we'll have some fun with one and sell the other. Now get a move on. Keep the head lights off."

The pirates jumped into the trucks and van, started their engines and roared off on the long haul up into the hills toward the caves that they called home.

Mykos and Kikon could barely breathe in the packed van. The other sailors, with their hands tied were unable to help themselves let alone the two companions.

All the men were terrified. Some prayed, others wept, and others lay in stunned silence till at last the van came to a screeching halt. The back doors of the van were yanked open and other brigands were standing ready to unload the human cargo. In a few minutes the ten survivors were lined up single file by the cave entrance. Thugs with rifles pointed at the sailors began to prod the men into the narrow dark opening of their hideout. Several spaces had been carved out of the rock which served as holding cells for captives. Barb wire and wooden slats provided security to keep the prisoners confined. The first cell was used to hold eight of the captives, Mykos and Kikon were shoved into the second room. They were still bound with chain which dug into their naked flesh making it impossible to lie down. They could only lean against one of the rough rock walls, their hands bound behind their back caused the shoulders to ache from the awkward position. After the prisoners were secured the pirates began unloading the arms shipment, dragging the heavy cumbersome boxes down the passage into the far reaches of the cavern.

Mykos and Kikon tried to doze but the constant clamor in the stone corridor made rest impossible.

At last the work was done and for awhile all was quiet in the cave. Only the sounds of men praying or whispering broke the stillness.

"I love you man." Whispered Mykos as the two were startled by the sounds of approaching pirates. The booming voice of Ali could be heard giving instructions but in a language that neither man understood.

Part Three

The cell gate was pushed open and Ali and a few of his band entered the cramped space.

"Well, which one shall be the night's entertainment? I wonder if you two are lovers?

Maybe you would like to watch each other?"

The two sailors faced their captor with eyes wide with fear, not understanding a word of what was being said.

"Strip them both and bring them to the store room."

Unable to resist Mykos and Kikon watched helplessly as their canvas trousers and underwear were yanked down around their legs and pulled off leaving them totally naked.

Their manhood shriveled in size from fear.

"Let's go."

Two of the pirates on each man, lifted and dragged the prisoners down the corridor. Their feet dragged along the jagged rock floor as they descended ever further into the cave. There were a few overhead electric lights strung on wire that partially illuminated the passage and cast hellish shadows on the sandstone walls. Mykos was first with Kikon following close behind. He saw his beloved's naked body, his powerful back, sculpted buttocks and strong young legs and nearly wept at the thought of what was to come. He was willing to do anything to save his friend, even die for him but doubted that he had much of a choice.

The term "wash room" was a cruel joke. The only nod was to a coiled hose used more for beating naked flesh then cleaning. It was in point of fact a torture chamber. At one end of the room sat a large straight back wooden chair bolted to the floor. A metal cot without a mattress was placed in the middle of the room with dirty well worn ropes hanging limp at the four corners. Suspended from the ceiling were hand cuffs attached to a chain threaded through a pulley overhead and operated by a winch midway down the wall.

A few feet away from the right wall was a hundred gallon oil drum, resting on its side. Imbedded in the floor on either side of the drum were thick iron eye bolts.

On a metal shelf were an assortment of pliers, alligator clips, needles and wire and whips.

"Put them up against the wall. Let's have a look."

As the two sailors were slammed against the rough rock other pirates began to assemble. Word had gone out that Ali was going to provide some entertainment tonight. Some men lit up cigars and cigarettes; other's brought in bottles of wine that had been salvaged from the Pratoclus.

The rowdy, drunken louts made themselves comfortable about the room as the sailor's escorts held the captives fast against the wall.

"Let's get a look at you." Ali stood a few inches from their pinned bodies and stared them up and down as though he were buying a prize Arabian stallion.

He grabbed Mykos under the chin and forced his jaw open to inspect his teeth then did the same to Kikon. Both men were sweating profusely, their eyes bugging out of their sockets in total terror.

"Good teeth on both of 'em, now lets look at their goods." He cast his eyes down as with his right hand he grabbed each sailor's ball sack and lifted it up slightly as if to test for the weight, like gagging a melon.

"hmmmmmmmm, both seem to be about the same, both of you will fetch a good price, more's the luck for you but my men need some fun so before we take you two to market let's see what you can take. Tie the short one up in the chair; let him watch what we do to his friend."

Mykos was dragged across the room and slammed into the high backed wooden chair. Ropes were quickly tied around his chest, wrists and ankles and tightened to the chair. A leather band was wrapped around his head and tied off behind the back of the chair forcing him to look straight ahead.

"Don't want you to miss anything."

Meanwhile Ali instructed others to throw Kikon over the barrel. His arms and legs were pulled tight and then tied with rope which was looped into the eye bolts in the floor.

His powerful perfectly formed white butt was displayed in all its glory making a tempting target first for the lash then for the repeated assaults of Ali's men who already were casting dice to see who would get to go first.

Mykos was unable to close his eyes but sat in his rigid confinement starring straight ahead at what was happening to his lover. He knew that begging for mercy would only add fuel to the fire that was between these pirates' legs, so he stayed still despite the tears that began streaking down his face.

Kikon found it hard to breathe as he was pulled so tightly over the drum. His chest and belly were pressed mercilessly against the metal which was rusted and jagged.

"Warm him up." Commanded Ali.

He went to the shelf and chooses a stout riding crop.

"Line up, you each get to take a turn. You boy," he said bending over to whisper in Kikon's ear, "if you yell out we'll jolt your friend with some juice from a field generator I have standing by, understand me boy?"

Kikon, through gritted teeth mumbles, "Yes."

"Wire the other one up."

The bandits practically fell over each other in their haste to pull out the field generator, get the alligator clips and wires untangled and attached.

Mykos gasped silently as each jagged metal clamp was fastened to his body. One was attached to his ball sack, one to tip of his penis and one to each of his tits. The stinging clips were like so many hornets but unlike the insect, the burn did not go away.

"Now, line up lets see if we can make this man scream."

The first in line took the riding crop raised it over his head and ran the twelve steps needed to land the first blow on the up turned ass. The short sharp crack of the leather against naked flesh reverberated around the cave. Kikon gritted his teeth and only the sudden tightening of his leg muscles and back indicated the pain that he was in. As soon as the crop was lifted a short red road across the butt appeared highlighted by tiny drops of blood. The first man handed the crop off to the second and then to the third till the young man's ass was cris-crossed with angry red welts. Sweat dripped down from his face, ran down the sides of the barrel and spattered across the room each time a blow was struck and his body jolted in spasms of pain yet never once did he cry out.

Mykos clamped his eyes shut but Ali who was watching for his reaction raised his had and slapped the sailor across the face.

"Keep you fukin' eyes open or your friend will get worse. Keep it up men, lay it on harder, and let's see if you can make this Greek lamb cry. Here, use the bull whip."

Drunk on wine and lust the pirates once again lined up but this time they stood well back from their victim, flicking the whip in grand fashion before it landed on target. The screaming pain in Kikon's ass was nearly unbearable. He needed to scream, he longed to cry out in agony yet he kept the image of his friend firmly in his head.

Mykos watched in horror as the beautiful rounded rump of his lover turned crimson with bloody welts. Perhaps if he screamed out, the pirates would turn their attention on him and leave his friend alone, if even for a minute.

"Noooooooooooo.   Stop, stop you're killing him. Stop."

The pirates were indeed distracted as they turned to face the young man bound tightly in the chair.

The cessation of pain gave Kikon the moment that he needed to pass out. His body went limp, draped over the barrel like the golden fleece.

Ali decided that this was enough, after all this piece of property must not be damaged beyond repair lest he not fetch a high price. Of course his men needed some release lest they start attacking each other so he let the men have their way with unconscious sailor.

Mykos could not bare the sight of his lover being raped over and over so he clamped his eyes shut and tried desperately to recall their summer days rolling on the beach in their private little cove.

Ali sat in a corner and watched his men have their way. He was too drunk to take part, besides his release came from watching the brutal beating of the captive. If he needed some personal pleasure there was always this one tied up in the chair. Maybe later he thought as he drifted into a drunken coma.

Part four

Davidis haunted the docks of Peraeus. He questioned every sailor back from the North Africa for news of the Patroclus and her crew. As they days dragged on in ignorance he realized that he must find a ship going to Libya, join her crew and once in port investigate on his own. The longing for his brother and even the sight of Kikon was more then he could endure. It was not too hard to find a berth on an old bucket that was bound for Tripoli and within days Davidis found himself shoveling coal in the boiler room of the Demeter a ship loaded with oil and crates of raw lambs wool for the carpet trade.

Stripped to the waist, covered in coal dust and sweating he labored endless hours in the bowels of the ship but the constant straining of his young muscles helped to get him back into shape after his dissipated life of ouzo and self pity.

And while Davidis shoveled coal, his brother and Kikon were riding in the back of trucks across desert mountain roads towards the slave market at Alankish. Their fellow crew mates had been sold off along the way to slave in the fields or mines but Ali knew valuable goods when he saw them and he knew his market as well. The Sheik of Alankish was a notorious sadist who admired male beauty above all else and would be willing to pay a fortune for these two Greek sailors.

Kikon has barely survived the beating and his ass was badly torn and battered from the repeated rapes but Ali made sure that medicine was provided and thanks to the tender administration of the loving Mykos, the sailor soon recovered.

At night the two men slept in each other's arms huddled against the cold desert night air shackled though they were to the side of the truck.

"Kikon, what are you thinking about." Whispered Mykos as camp settled down for sleep.

"Mykos, what if the sell us to separate masters? I don't think I could survive with out you."

"I feel the same way."

"We have got to figure out a way to escape."

The pirates caravan arrived in Alankish near midnight. The trucks pulled up to a broken down hotel not far from the slave market. Ali and his men made their way inside, leaving the two sailors secured inside the truck.

"Mykos, we've got to make our move and soon before we're separated."

"I know and the word is that we might end up in the Emir's hands, with all his guards and security we would be killed if we tried to escape."

"God man, I wish we were back in Pareaus."

"We'll get home, don't worry. We'll make it." And he leaned over as far as the ropes would allow and kissed Mykos tenderly first on the eyes, then on the lips.

———————————————————

Davidis jumped ship the first chance he had after docking in Tripoli. He was well used to handling himself in bars and drinking with the best of 'em so it was not to difficult for him to eventually pry out information about the crew of the Patroclus. One drunken old pirate with only one hand, a victim of Ali's rage was only too happy to pass along what information he had. He told the young Greek sailor that he had heard that two crewmen from the doomed vessel were being taken to Alankish to be sold the Emir, a sadist who used up young men in his dungeons for his pleasure notorious then threw their bones to bleach in the scorching desert sun.

Davidis' blood ran to ice at the thought of his brother and Kikon being doomed to such a terrible end. He must find a way to get to Alankish.

———————————————————————

At first light the back end of the truck clanked open. Anxious hands grabbed the sailor's legs and dragged them out the rear of the vehicle. Rifle barrels were used to prod the two men, groggy from sleep and stiff from being trussed all night. To the gate leading to the Emir's compound. Uniformed guards gave the filthy brigands and their two walking pieces of meat close scrutiny then unlocked the door and allowed them to pass.

The court yard was dark, swarming with flies and smelled of dung. In one corner of the square stood a well worn T shaped cross with chains and cuffs. Resting against an adjacent wall was a St. Andrews cross.

The Emir Omar Ben Sulimiman had been told of Amir's arrival the previous night. He was bursting with curiosity to get a glimpse of these two Greek sailors.

He was a ruthless war lord who ruled his tiny desert town

with an iron fist. A few loyal Turk mercenaries kept the town in line. These men also shared Omar's sadistic nature and enjoyed nothing more then watching handsome men suffer and beg for their lives. Sometimes they would let them live, usually gelding them first then turning them into slaves to work at menial jobs till they outgrew their usefulness.

Omar planned on paying a good price if he liked what he saw. It was always good to keep Amir as a friend and supplier. He had access to the coast, shipping and truck lanes that would provide an endless supply of fresh strong bucks.

Davidis took what little money he had from his work on the Demeter, bought a bullet riddled jeep left over from WW2, filled it with petrol and headed south for Alankish.

Mykso and Kikon were forced to kneel on the filthy cobblestone to await the arrival of Omar. They were not aware that he was standing at an upper window with one of his favorite companions, the Turk Otho who was an expert in the fine art of torture.

"What do you think Otho?"

"From what I can tell from up here, they look strong enough. Good backs at any rate. Let's go get a closer look."

Omar turned and with slow measured steps made his way down the stairs and into the courtyard with Otho following close behind.

"Amir, my good friend, how wonderful to see you. And what have you brought me today?"

"Two fine specimens from Greece oh exalted one. These two sailors are strong, handsome and fit for years of service.

Come, get a closer look." And with that Amir lead the Sheik over to Mykos.

"Life up your head boy. Let your new master see your face. Quite splendid, yes? Perfect lips and mouth, perfect teeth and eyes to get lost in." Amir grabbed the front of Mykos' shirt, popped the few remaining buttons and yanked the shirt down revealing the young man's chest.

"And take a look at the chest, the fine toned muscles, and perfect tits. What could be more splendid?"

"Yes, I agree, totally. I will take him. Let him be tied to the T cross."

"At once my friend. You two, do it."

Two of the Amir's henchmen pulled Mykos up by his hair and dragged to the T shaped cross. His arms were uncuffed long enough to stretch his arms along the cross beam and secure them in the manacles.

"Strip him the rest of the way. Let's get a look at what is between his legs."

"While your men are preparing that one, let's take along this other sailor."

"Indeed."

Again the two men stood a few inches away from the kneeling captive.

"Lift your face dog."

"Ah, this one is even more handsome I see."

"I quite agree, therefore I will have to charge a slightly higher price but since you are such a good costumer, shall we say one thousand drachmas for the pair?"

"I won't argue. Go inside and see my agent. He'll give you your money. Let's get this one stripped and spread eagled, I can hardly wait to get started."

Two of Turk mercenaries brutally grabbed Kikon by the under arms and got him to a standing position the dragged him over to the X cross. While one soldier stationed himself behind the trembling sailor the other undid the chains and positioned the captive's arms along the top part of the cross for shackling. A sharp sudden knee to the groin and Kikon's leg were splayed open and attached to the bottom of the cross.

"Beautiful sight." Omar said practically drooling with anticipation.

"Get me a knife, let's cut this one's rags off."

Before Omar's words were completed one of the Turks handed him a fierce hunting knife.

The Sheik took the knife and clenched it in his fist, raised it in the air and advanced towards Kikon whose eyes filled with terror. Mykos looked on helplessly from his cross wondering how long this agony of terror and physical pain could possibly last.

"Don't be afraid my little sailor man. I just want to make you more comfortable by getting out of these confining louse infested rags. Here, I shall start at your waist band and cut the fabric, just so." And so Omar began to slowly slice through the tattered fabric like he was unpeeling an exotic fruit. First one pant leg then the other was cut then to drop down to the stone beneath. A simple yank on the undergarments left Kikon totally naked. His balls had ascended into his scrotum, as though in hiding. Even his prodigious penis seemed to shrivel at the mere thought of what was to come next. The young man tried to swallow but his mouth was so dry from fright that he could barely breathe.

He bent his head to the left to see Mykos, as though to take strength from his friend but the terror he saw in his friend's eyes only made him suffer the more.

Davidis drove the rattling old truck like a race car driver leaving swirling dust and flying pebbles in his wake. He knew from all that he had heard that if he was going to save his twin and beloved Kikon he must travel like the wind. Tears coursed down his strong handsome face as he contemplated what his life would be like were he to lose these two men from his life. On the truck seat beside him was a machine gun that he had stolen from a drunken soldier in the last town. He had also managed to procure a hand grenade from a loathsome creature he had met in a hash joint. He had to let the man suck him off but it was worth it.

The desert sun finally began to desend, casting long cool shadows across the landscape, and then in the distance he could make out the mud and brick walls of Omar's compound.

Omar stood before the naked sailor and with his right hand reached down and grabbed the scrotum that was dangling so temptingly between the strong hairy legs. The velvet softness and heft of the encased gonads sent a thrill deep into the Sheiks gut. He would enjoy making the man suffer through his manhood. He removed a two foot length of cord from his pocket and with practiced fingers quickly tied and separated the two balls nestled in their pouch. Kikon took short staccato breaths at each yank, pull and rough manipulation as the tying went forward. The Greek was certain that he was being prepared for castration.

Davidis pulled his truck off the road and drove down into a gully hoping that it would not be seen by any lookout from the compound. He then waited till the sun had set before venturing towards the walls. Counting on the element of surprise and hoping that Omar would be too distracted by the diversion of having two Greek gods at his mercy to pay attention to a new person seeking shelter in his little town.

His hopes were born out as he entered through an open gate in the town's wall. A few rough residents were huddled around the gate that led to Omar's "palace." Brought there by the sound of a man being flogged. The screams of the victim penetrated the stone wall and filled the night air. Davidis at once recognized the sound of the man's voice, it was Mykos.

In the courtyard, Omar decided that a good chest whipping was a fine way to warm up the shorter sailor as the night was growing cold. He was standing before the bruised and bloody sailor, a nine stranded flogger in his hand preparing to strike for the twentieth time when the explosion at the gate knocked him to the ground.

A great blast of sand, stone, splintered wood and nails burst into the court yard followed by a blinding flash of machine gun fare that riddled the Turk mercenaries who were up and running for their weapons. Bullets ricocheted off the flag stone like bouncing hail, one stray bullet striking and penetrating Omar's right eye. He screamed in agony, blindly trying to seek cover but a second bullet, this one aimed by Davidis slammed into and exited through his fat neck. He dropped like a piece of dead meat.

Davidis, Mykos and Kikon used the money they had found in Omar's store room, a considerable sum, to pay for salvaging and repair of the Protoculus. In a few weeks the battered freighter left the harbor, Kikon in command with his two first mates, Mykos and Davidis by his side.

Tank Books

Old Man's Revenge

The last time old man Higgins saw his son Jake alive, the sun was just coming up over the San Mateo ridge. Jake was his only child, a strapping lad of twenty-three. The two men raised a few head of cattle and farmed a small plot of land, just enough to get by. It was a hard cruel existence and Jake longed to get away. Every time a Texas Ranger or stray cavalry squad rode by his yearning to be free grew another ten feet. He knew he could be a terrific law man or pony soldier. He rode well, was plenty strong and a crack shot to boot. He had grown up mostly alone as the closest other ranch was nearly ten miles away and even there dwelled only a few girls, no fellas his own age. Most of his days from the time he was a little tike were spent on horseback. Life in the saddle was grueling but Jake loved horses and the desert air. The feel of the sun on his bronzed chest as he lay on a rock down along the edge of the Rio on lazy afternoons or the wind blowing through his long wheat colored hair as he rode bare chest across the desert was almost enough to ease his loneliness.

The closest town between the Higgins' place and Albuquerque was a grease spot of a place called Santa Marta some ten miles north. It had been named after a long deserted Spanish mission and it was there he was headed that last morning. Santa Marta had a saloon called Sheri's, a sheriff's office, a feed store, a pony express exchange, a little church with graveyard and a broken down rooming house. Every rancher and stray cowboy in a hundred mile radius passed through here once a month for supplies or to get drunk on rot gut and get laid. Like rats feeding off the refuse of this miserable town were outlaws and misfits of every imaginable stripe. Santa Marta was more like an outpost of Hell then a town.

"Jake, don't forget the fat-back and some two-penny nails."

"I won't Pa. Be back before dark." Jake with his dark blue bandana tied around his neck shouted over his shoulder as he snapped the horses' reigns.

Old Man Higgins stood on the porch sadly watching his son's back as it vanished down the road. He new Jake was ready to strike out on his own. This was no life for a good looking young buck. With a heavy sigh the old rancher turned and slouched off to the barn.

It was well after sunset that the old man started to worry but he figured maybe a wagon wheel busted or a horse threw a shoe. Lots of good reasons for his son to be late he told himself. Exhausted from another day of endless chores the old man soon fell asleep at the kitchen table. It wasn't till the barnyard roster started his crowing that he woke.

"Jake" he called as he stood up and walked the few steps to his son's room. He opened the door and saw nothing but a made up bed.

"Damn it to hell, where is that boy?" he said out loud. "Somethin' ain't right. Maybe the boy was just sowin' some wild oats with a gal or two from the saloon, lost track of time."

With these and other more dire thoughts Higgins made some coffee and started the day's work.

Long about sun down the second day and still no sign of Jake. It was time to saddle up the horse and ride into town, go see the sheriff and see what was up. The agony of not knowing was becoming more then the old man could stand.

At first light Higgins saddled his horse and rode off to Santa Marta. As he made his way down a dried up arroyo he spotted in the distance five or six crows circling in the clear blue sky. Probably some dead animal he told him self, willing it to be so as he spurred his horse on in the direction of the birds. Coming up over a low rise he saw in the distance that which he dreaded more then anything in the world. There lying face down in the dust was the naked battered body of his only son. His back, ass and legs were covered in bruises and angry welts and most horrible of all, sticking out of his rectum was a dried up branch from a salt wood tree. Higgins let out a war hoop of rage and despair that echoed across the desert. He fell from his horse and stumbled like a drunken mad man across to Jake, gently removed the obscene marker, turned is son over and cradled the dead boy in his arms.

It was a grim sight to see, the old man leading a horse with a body draped over the saddle making his way down the main street of town. Higgins had thrown a saddle blanket over his son but it barely covered Jake's back. Jake's nakedness was all too apparent as the few towns' people and sheriff stepped outside to bare witness to the sad cortege.

"Mr. Higgins, is that your son?" Sheriff Connor asked as he approached the old man.

Sheriff Connor had been around too many years, had seen too much to care anymore though he had to admit that he felt a slight lump in his throat as he gazed at the farmer's tear streaked face.

Higgins just nodded yes, unable to utter any words.

Connor turned to the few men standing in the crowd, "Give

him a hand. Take the boy into my office."

Higgins stood by and watched silently as Jake was lifted off the horse.

"Come on with me Higgins, get you a whiskey. Then you can tell me all about it."

"Yes Sheriff."

After downing three double shots Higgin's spoke haltingly of all he had seen.

"Well, we will find whoever did this awful thing and hang 'em up high, don't you worry about that. We'll form a possy right away while the trail is fresh. You check into the roomin' house, tell Bertha the town will pay and try to get some rest."

"Thank you, Sheriff Connor."

Connor strode out of the saloon and went about the business of getting a few volunteers to help with the search doubting all the while that they would have much luck.

In these parts there were a lot of sick drunk scum or maybe it was a bunch of Indians that got into some stolen whiskey. But he told the old man he would try.

The possy rode out within the hour but returned before sun down. There were a few tracks but the wind and drifting sand erased the horror, horse and boot track, blood and torn fabric. It was with much sadness that the Sheriff broke the news to Old Man Higgins.

"Maybe somebody saw or heard somethin', never know. We'll get the bastards that done this. We'll see to the buryin' in the mornin', get the preacher man to say a few nice words, damn shame Mr. Higgins, mighty damn shame."

Jason rolled over yawned and stretched his six foot five frame while rubbing the sleep from his eyes. A night of drinking at Sherri's had left him a little under the weather but hell, after driving cattle from Santa Fe to St. Louis and a long ride to New Mexico he was in need of rest and a roll in the hay. His right hand reached across the bed and touched the vacant pillow by his side. He gently smiled remembering the young rancher he had met the night before. How they shared a few drinks and talked into the wee hours of the morning. Of how their knees touched under the bar, gently, haltingly cautiously at first feeling that first thrill of returned pressure when thigh meets thigh, when a silent message between two occurs that yes, I want you. He remembered leaning over to Jake and whispering, "Lets get outta here; I got a room at the boardin' house across the street." And how the two of them had walked out of Sheri's, proud and tall, not paying any attention to drunks and gamblers stares. If he closed his eyes he could see young Jake lying on the old brass bed, arms down by his side, still wearing his shirt, Levi's and boots. And then there was that wonderful moment of discovery as Justin straddled him on the bed. The feel of his buckskin shirt as he slowly undid the buttons and peeled back the hide revealing that smooth muscled chest, of leaning down to take his right tit in his mouth letting his tongue caress and tease that pink rose bud. And then the wonderful moment when he undid the belt buckle and opened Jake's pants, placing his hand down deep inside the waste band as it searched for the growing excitement between Jake's legs. Then the boots came off revealing the rancher's long slender feet, the pulling down of trousers and under ware the first sight of the rigid cock, so slender, so rigid, so glowing with pulsing blood, the two balls seeming to churn in their sack and then the sublime moment as he took the head of young man's prick in his mouth feeling Jake's body arch driving the rigid member deeper into Jason's throats. How well he remembered all of this, of their two bodies now naked, entwined in each others arms and legs. Jason all bronzed, hair covered chest and belly, his own rigid pole encased in a forest of thick black crotch hair all this contrasted against the paler and smoother form of the man below him. These memories excited Jason again as he reached down and pumped his spike stroking it up and down and remembering the beautiful young man that he had possessed and been possessed. They had parted the day before; Jake had insisted that he must get back to the ranch lest his father worry but promising to get back to town again as soon as possible. Perhaps Jake might join Jason on another cattle drive, all things to talk about the next time they met. As a small remembrance Jake left his blue bandana with Jason which Jason now clutched to his face inhaling its scent.

With a long low sigh Jason came in a series of powerful spurts. It was time to get up and get some vitals. The wash basin was on a stand near a window facing the main street of town. As he splashed water on his face and chest he glanced through the faded curtains just in time to see some men carrying a blanket covered body into the sheriff's office.

An involuntary shudder shot down his spine. Couldn't be Jake he said out loud but nevertheless a sick fear seemed to grip his belly. Might as well go down and see what's up. He dressed quickly, stuffed Jake's blue scarf in his trouser pocket and hurried down the rickety old stairs. The white hot sun and the dry oven like heat hit him like a brick.

"Hey mister, they just brought in Jake Higgins, dead." This news alert was from a wizened old drunk with a wad of tobacco in his jaw sitting on the boarding house stoop.

Jason took a step back like he could somehow reverse time

by moving in reverse.

He'd really liked the guy, first time he had felt something other then pure lust but the urge of preservation was a mighty strong urge.

In less the ten minutes he had his saddle bag packed and was a quarter mile out of town.

Old Man Higgins sat in the saloon getting drunker by the minute. The midnight hour had struck on the bar clock. Three saddle tramps sat huddled in the corner playing cards. The farmer through blurred eyes watched them intently as they shuffled, dealt and bet, cursing, spitting and drinking. These fellas looked like the kind he needed. Tough, no good sons a bitches is what he wanted. He was willing to pay almost any price to get revenge for his boy. Maybe he thought these three might be interested in helping him track down and punish his boy's murderer?

Holding on the backs of chairs he cautiously made he was over.

"You fellas wanna make some cash? "

"What you talking about old man?" said Gomez, the oldest of the three. A livid scar ran from the corner of his right eye down across his lips and ending at the base of his chin giving his face the look of some goblin from Hell. The other two, Pedro and Sancho were only slightly less ugly though forty years of drinking, fighting and riding had left them looking as though there were made of aged cracked leather. Thick black stubble and bushy black moustaches said, stay away.

"I got a proposition for you three. You know what that word means, proposition."

"Yea" was answered in unison.

"You heard about that young man that was found dead this morning? Well he was my son. I want some help finding the heathen piece of shit that did that to my boy and I want him alive. I want him to suffer long and hard before I send him to hell. You three interested in helpin'? Make it worth your while I will. Fifty dollars a piece."

"How we know you got that kind of money old man."

"Oh I got it alright. I got a ranch ten miles from here, every body around here knows me, knows I got money. You can ask. I don't mind."

The men huddled around the table for a few minutes speaking in Spanish.

"Yea old man, we're in."

"Good" Higgins sighed as he took a seat at the table.

Sancho was the first to speak.

"Ya know old man, we comes to think we saw this cowboy with your boy last night. Saw 'em leavin' together we did. Watched him drinkin' and talkin' over there at the bar, gettin' good-n-soused they was."

Pedro added, "Si I remember. Didn't see the young fella again but this morning when you brought the body in and I was takin' a leak I saw that cowboy fella high tale it out of here, headed North he was."

"We gotta go after 'em now."

"No Signor, to dark, wait till first light then we go." Said Gomez, obviously the leader.

"Besides, we need to get some rest and equipment."

"Get plenty of rope, tent spikes and a jar of molasses" Higgins instructed through his slurred speech.

Sancho added, "And mucho tequila."

The three tramps had lived long enough in the desert and heard and seen enough of Indian punishment to know what was in store for this cowboy if they ever caught him. Their exchanged leers were enough to send shivers down the spine of anyone watching but the bar tender was passed out and the four were alone.

Jason managed to travel a good five miles before his horse went lame.

"Damn it to hell." he yelled at the top of his lungs. This old palomino had been with him for a good long time. He sure didn't want to shoot the animal but then he couldn't stand the thought of him suffering in the heat turning into food for the buzzards. He waited till morning hoping against hope that the horse would recover but no such luck. As the sun started to glow red in the sky he loaded up his rifle and with a tear in his eye shot the horse once through the skull.

"What was that?" Old Man Higgins shouted to Miguel

"Signor, it came from over that ridge, maybe our hombre shot a snake. Come muchazos."

Jason knew it was at least a two day walk to get to the next outpost and in the blazing heat of day he would never make it.

Best thing to do was find a tree or big rock and rest in the shade till evening.

Another half hours walking brought him to a lone struggling box wood tree with a few sparsely leafed limps, enough to provide a small amount of shade. He leaned up against the rough bark, drank a short swig from his canteen and tried to get some shut eye. With the heat and wind whistling across the desert he soon fell into a quiet gentle sleep. And in his slumber a dream came to him. He and Jake were riding along together headed south towards Mexico. They were riding bare back, with their shirts off feeling the warmth of the sun on their naked flesh. Up ahead was the gently rolling Rio Grande. Jason spurred his mount on ahead to ford the river and as he turned back to check on his companion he fell from his horse into blackness.

"Stand him up."

"Si Mr. Higginis."

"What the hell?" Jason gasped as he slowly recovered from the blow of a riffle butt to his gut. Struggling like a wild bronco he desperately tried to fight off the onslaught of the three drunken thugs. But outnumbered and taken by surprise he was no match for the brutes despite his powerful build. In but a few minutes he was pinned down flat on his back. Sancho and Miguel held his arms while Pedro sat on his lower legs.

Old Man Higgins stood a few feet away passively observing the defeated cowboy.

With a look of total contempt and loathing the farmer moved forward a step and said in a venom filled whisper, "Strip him."

"Si Signor" responded the three.

Jason franticly bucked and writhed but to no avail. Pedro unhooked a hunting knife he had stuck in his belt.

"Take your time." Higgins instructed, "I want him to last a long time, let him know what is in store for him."

"Old man you're crazy, what the hell is this all about, is this about your kid? Listen old man, you gotta believe me, please I really like Jake."

"Damn you to hell, don't you mention his name you sticking snake."

"But I'm telling the truth, please we just met the night before, we liked it each other a lot, thought about joining up together."

Higgins stepped a few feet forward and despite his advanced years kicked the cowboy hard in the ribs. The jolt of pain was intense. Jason thought he must have cracked a rib.

Each breath now caused a sharp jab like a knife in ribs.

"What did I tell you, boy?"

Jason looked hard at the livid expression on the old man's face and knew he would get nowhere but maybe if he pleaded with these three Mexicans.

"You men, you know I saw you in the saloon, you saw I liked the guy, tell the old man please."

"Shut up gringo, save your strength."

And with those words Pedro inserted the tip of his knife at the collar button of Jason's shirt and began a slow move downward popping each button, relishing the look of terror on the young man's face. Then with a few deft slices he cut through the shoulder seams while Sancho and Miguel pulled at the fabric till Jason lay stripped to the waist.

His chests hair was now matted from sweat and desert dust. He tried to take deep breaths but the cracked rib made each intake of air agony.

"All the way, strip him buck naked" was Higgin's next instruction.

Again the tip of the ten inch blade was placed at Jason's belly button then slowly the blade sliced through the crotch of the captive's pants. With a few more cuts and much yanking and pulling of fabric Jason soon found him self stark naked. His usually impressive cock and balls now exposed to these cut throats had pulled up into his groin as though hiding in fear.

Higgins looked down at the shrinking manhood and with an evil smile said, "get some raw hide and tie up his balls and prick."

Pedro jumped up and rummaged around his saddle bag till he found a three foot length of raw hide which he deftly tied around the ball sack and looped a noose around the base of Jason's pole and pulled tight before tying the loose ends into a tight knot. The raw hide now trapped the blood flow to the organ. In a matter of seconds Jason's manhood stood out and up now a livid color of purple.

"What are you going to do? I swear to God I done nothing to your son. You gotta believe me; please I don't want to die."

"Is that what my son said to you? Please I don't want to die? Did you listen to him? Did you show pity to him? Tell me damn you."

"You've got the wrong man." Jason pleaded and cried out but to no avail.

"Drag him over into the sun. Sancho get the spikes."

Sancho did as told as the other two dragged the frantic cowboy kicking and pleading out into the burning desert sun. Sancho found a rock with which to pound the four spikes into place positioning them as the other two hombres held Jason spread eagled. Try has he did to kick and buck the experienced tramps were too much for him.

In short order the cowboy was tied tight with raw-hide laces tightly entwined to the four wooden stakes. The blinding glare of the sun and the dust from the hot desert floor filled his mouth, nostrils and eyes with burning agony. He struggled yet more wildly trying to dislodge the spikes but to no avail. He heaved his chest up, tried to bend his legs, thrusting his pelvis into the air, his tightly tied manhood flapping against his lower belly and thighs. Higgins and the Mexicans passed a bottle of tequila and with grim satisfaction, watched as their quarry wasted his energy in his futile struggle to get free.

At last, totally exhausted, Jason fell back into the sand resigned at least for the moment to save his rapidly dwindling strength.

"Sit down boys, drink up. We got all day; let this heathen bastard enjoy the sun. Take a little siesta why don't you? Get rested up for some fun tonight" said Higgins.

"Si Signore," all around as the bottle was passed. The four found some shade and made themselves comfortable as the cowboy broiled in the sun. Jason felt as though his entire body was under a flame. The sun beat relentlessly down on his sweat drenched body. It seared into his eyelids stinging like a thousand bees. His lips soon became dry and cracked liked a dried up arroyo. His mouth turned into a giant ball of cotton as his tongue swelled. Then came the ants. First he felt the slightest crawling sensation on his right foot. Then another and another as the tiny but voracious ants, attracted by the moisture and the sent of man sweat began their explorations. One after another their attacking army formed, soon a battalion long line marched slowly up the inside of his right leg headed for his sweat soaked balls and rigid cock. Was he to be eaten alive? He slowly came back to his senses from his sun induced comma. The expression on Jason's face was one of total horror. He tried to scream but his mouth was to dry to make to much sound. A dry hacking cough was all he could muster but it was enough to arouse the old man who stood and walked over to the spread eagled young man.

"I see you have some visitors. I saw once a man's flesh eaten totally off his foot before he died. Died screamin' like a mad man he did. I want you to think of my beautiful Jake as those hungry ants start to devour your cock and balls.

"No please for the love of god..." Jason managed to whisper through his dust filled lips.

He thrashed his head back and forth trying to blot out the ever increasing pain of the constant biting; he tried lifting his head and slamming it back down hard onto the hard ground to knock himself out but this also to no avail.

Higgins watched the cowboy's face contort in pain. An idea passed through his brain, something he had scene the Indians do once to captured cavalry scout.

"You, Sancho, the rest of you, come over him, you had enough tequila now, go ahead piss on this bastard, piss in his mouth, he looks thirsty but also soak his cock and balls while your at it. The ants like a little piss too."

With much stumbling, laughing and back slapping the three managed to stand, pull their meat out of their pants and let forth three streams of hot stinking, blinding piss.

Jason nearly wretched from the acrid smell and yet enjoying a brief respite from the stinging insects. But after a few moments the ants began to bite with even great fury.

It was soon clear to the old man that if it didn't stop soon the cowboy would die of poison from the bites and he had so much more he wanted to do before he sent this fella to hell.

"Ok boys, brush those buggers of him. We got more fun ahead."

The three knelt down and with hands roughly brushed the invading army away.

"Bring some water, let him have a taste. Don't want him dropping dead yet" the old man instructed.

"Si Signor" said Sancho who quickly brought his canteen and let drop a few pressure sprinkles of water on Jason's parched and bleeding lips.

It was enough to bring him back into agonizing consciousness.

"Kill me please. I did nothing before God I swear, please" he whispered.

"Gather some leaves and twigs you three, stick 'em between his legs and under his arms. I got a flint in my saddle bag. You know what to do." Higgins next order was carried out a little less slowly this time as the level of alcohol clouded their brains and slowed their actions. At last the kindling was found and mounded and jabbed into Jason's hairy arm pits and clumsily stacked around his engorged ball sack. The cowboy's eyes seemed to bulge clear out of his head and the horror of what was happening to him. His heart was beating so fast and hard it could each thump was visible through his tightly stretched rib cage.

Once the fuel was in place Old Man Higgins on arthritic knees knelt down by Jason's head. He leaned in close to right side and struck the flint a few times till sparks ignited a few dried leaves which quickly caught and burst into a puff a flame. The orange dragon burned down a twig that was embedded into the tender arm pit. In an instant the thick patch of black hair smoldered, sparked and burst into a screaming frenzied shriek of pain.

Jason opened his mouth and let out a blood curdling scream the force of which sent a spray of caked blood and mucus into the air. The old man sat back on his haunches and smiled with satisfaction.

"This is for you Jake. I hope you hear these screams in heaven."

Higgins reached across Jason's out stretched body and lit the kindling on his left side, a similar sequence of smoke, sparks, flame and agony.

Once the arm pit flames subsided Higgins managed to crawl down between the cowboys wishbone like legs.

"Hey old man, you sure know how to make a man scream. Want some tequila old man?" asked Pedro.

But the farmer was lost in a sea of retribution and could hear or see nothing save the suffering young man before him.

Taking his place between Jason's legs, he carefully adjusted the leaves and sticks mounding them high around the deep purple sack and rod. Then carefully striking the flint till a leaf caught flame he moved back to watch as the flames descended the twigs and headed for their target. As the fire began to plaster the sensitive nut sack Jason let out one last scream that rent the air like a clap of thunder. This cry of agony sure would be heard in heaven. Overcome at last from the pain and exposure Jason drifted into that place beyond pain, beyond hope, beyond life. His final moment a gentle sigh of release.

"Hey old man, looks like he's dead." Sancho said as he staggered, bottle in hand over to the body. A couple of quick jabs to Jason's side confirmed his thought.

"Old man, me and the boys, we have somethin' to tell you, ass. It was us." He whispered in the Old Man's ears.

"What?" Higgins was lost in thought and unable to comprehend the words.

"It was us, Pedro, Miguel and me. We done it good to that pretty ass son of yours. We saw him commin' by the saloon in the morning, thought we'd have some fun. So you see Old Man, you gonna go to Hell yourself for taken the life of this cowboy. How you like that Old Man?"

For a moment Higgins was caught unable to breathe. A giant vice clamped over his heart sending waves of excruciating pain into his gut, down his arms and into his brain. He tried to stand but the pain was too great. He slumped down to the ground, unable even to cry out, taking a last long futile gasp for air as he fell face forward into the dry desert sand.

"Pass the bottle."

An Iron Chair

Count Umberto Orsini stood behind the soot blackened, blood stained iron chair, which sat firmly bolted into the stone floor. His long aristocratic fingers gently caressed the tiny pointed pyramids that covered the back of the torture device. He caressed each of the sharp points as though it were some exotic fur from the Far East. Soon Carlo Begnalio would occupy this chair. Carlo, the favorite of the peasants and the nobles alike. Carlo so handsome and strong would soon be stripped naked, slammed into the spike-encrusted chair while coals placed beneath the seat were fanned into glowing ingots of excruciating agony. Yes, Carlo would pay dearly for his treachery.

The Orsini family had spies in every part of the peninsula including the Vatican. Word had already arrived at Castle Orsini from the court of Pope Marcellus that Carlo had begged for an audience to complain of the Orsini family's business dealings. What an outrage Umberto fumed. Yes, he would pay dearly for this and for the double sin of leaving him for study in Rome. This abandonment was the worst affront of all.

Umberto stood there remembering Carlo and their years together as boys. And those first awkward moments as teenagers when they began to explore each others bodies. How delicious those first fumbling, spent out in the forest or by some shady brook. The feel of Carlo's smooth bronzed skin that covered such perfectly honed muscle, the taste of his flesh as Orsini ran his tongue around each nipple, the musk of the young man's crotch as he placed his lips around the head of his friend's cock. He could close his eyes and imagine every sublime moment of their first lovemaking, the wondrous sensation as he slid his member into the gripping black velvet smoothness of Carlo's ass, the almost instant shudder of release that followed as he wrapped his arms around the chest and pulled Carlo tightly impaling him on his throbbing rod. Yes, these were such wonderful memories.

But then the years went by so quickly. Carlo went off to Rome to study law, Umberto staying to oversee his father's, the Old Count Alfredo Orsini, lands. It was during those long lonely months waiting for Carlo to return that dark shadows began to torment his soul. Those hungers could only be satiated here in this very room.

How vividly he remembered the first time he entered this place, the torture chamber, the centerpiece of Alfredo's power. He must have been twenty-one at the time he mused. His father had accused some stable lad of crippling a favorite horse. Alfredo thought it high time his son should see how to deal with peasants, to initiate him into that powerful elixir of watching a man suffer the torments of hell.

Over the years the young man had heard the whispers in dark halls or out in the fields of some missing young man from the village or surrounding farms. Adding to the mystery were the pitiful screams echoing throughout the castle and seeming to emanate from the bowels of the dungeon. These rumors and cries had both sickened and excited him in equal measure. He wondered if he also had been possessed by some devil that gave him a thrill witnessing the suffering of others. The images in the church, the unimaginable suffering of the Saints, in particular the muscular and naked St. Sebastian, the saints grilled or flayed, racked or crucified riveted his attention during the most tedious sermons and prayers. Yes, when his father suggested his son attend the punishment he leapt at the opportunity. The pleasure of anticipation was heightened by the fact that the lad in question, one Francesco by name, was a particularly stunning young man worthy to serve as a model for Signor Caravaggio. Francesco with the long wavy dark hair, coal black eyes, and smile that would warm the coldest night, the muscular chest and arms that he showed off striped to the waist and glistening with sweat in the summer as he cleaned the stable or outdoors walking some horse. How he longed to posses that beauty but the vast chasm between their ranks made such a liaison out of the question. Now, he could at least watch the man suffer. Perhaps his father might let him wield the whip or irons himself. The thought sent a rush of engorging blood into his groin causing his cock to swell and his balls to turn.

Umberto drifted back to that glorious night when, after dinning with his father and a few local blood sucking petty officials and an assortment of lascivious clerics, the two had made their way down into the dungeon with only a smoking torch to light their way.

He could even remember the smell of the urine, soot, sweat and blood stained passage as though it were some exotic fragrance from Arabia, giving him that heightened sense of expectation of wonderful things to come. How thrilling to hear the sound of their boot clad feet echoing off the vaulted stone surface, like the overture of some Monteverdi opera. Then the rough-hewn door crisscrossed with black iron bars slowly opening, the curtain going up on the stage, the leading man already in place, standing with arms stretched high above his head, wrists bound in rough hemp that was threaded into the wheel of a pulley high above his head. His white peasant shirt torn and blood spattered was open to reveal a few black chest hairs peaking up just below his neck and his grime encrusted pantaloons full of rips and tares revealing just a hint or two of the two powerful legs underneath were nothing to the excitement that the sight of his bare perfectly formed feet gave the young Umberto.

"Francesco, this is my son, Umberto but I believe that you know each other. Umberto has come to witness the punishment for those foolish enough to be careless in my service. You have caused the death of my prized stallion and for this offense you shall suffer like you made that magnificent beast suffer."

"Signore, please it was not my fault. He tripped on a gofer hole in the paddock and broke his leg. I loved that animal like he was my own. I would rather break my own leg then cause harm to that horse," Francesco's torrent of words gushed forth but were heeded not by Count Alfredo who was busy instructing his chief torturer, one Davide by name. He was an ugly bastard from Milan who had learned his trade from the hands of the Spanish Inquisition.

Umberto sat on a stone bench recessed into the wall. Here he could take in the entire chamber, a front row seat.

Francesco watched in fear as Davide took two lengths of rope which he used to bind each of the prisoner's ankles then took the ends of each rope and tossed them over a cross beam in the ceiling. With a few skillful pulls, Francesco's legs were lifted off the floor. The bare and vulnerable soles of his feet now even with his shoulder. The bastinado would begin.

"See Umberto, we begin with the feet." Alfredo whispered in nearly reverential tone as David prepared the prisoner.

The whistling sound of the bamboo rod shipped from the Far East for this singular purpose was split at the ends. Signor Davide's prized possession. He stood before his target, the white bare feet looking so strong and yet so tender. What a pleasing sight to Carlo as he imagined how it would have been to suck on this manly toes but his fantasy was cut short, first by the whirring sound of the bamboo slashing through the rancid air then the sharp crack of wood against Francesco's high arches. The split ends of the rod cut like sharpened knives. Francesco cried out in shock at the lacerating agony.

Again and again, the bamboo rod whistled and landed, whistled and landed turning the soles of the wretched stable boy into a mass of bleeding welts. Each strike brought greater agony, cuts into welts, lacerations in raw muscle. Soon Francesco was screaming with wild abandon, his cries echoing off the stonewalls like a man suffering in the depths of hell. But nature or God at last came to the rescue rendering surcease from suffering in momentary unconsciousness.

"Bravo Maestro Davide, Bravo. Now, wake him up and strip him."

"Yes Count."

"Are you enjoying this Umberto?"

"Yes" Umberto said quietly but with a new voice, the voice of man deeply in love.

"Good."

Alfredo crossed the chamber, took a seat by his son on the bench, and watched with great interest as Davide went about his business.

First he took a of pitcher of water and poured it slowly over Francesco's face bringing the lad back to wakefulness then lowered the ankle restraints till the prisoner was standing foursquare on the rough floor. The exposed torn flesh against the jagged edges of the floor's stone tiles caused another wave of total agony that like a tidal wave started in the soles of his feet, moved up his legs, his thighs into his gut. He nearly wretched from the pain.

The torturer stood a few inches from the trembling stable boy and with deft hands shredded his shirt in two, leaving the torn fabric to drop to the floor. Next, he brutally yanked down his pantaloons and under garment roughly moving, them down his legs and off over his lacerated feet. At each move, Francesco let out a small groan of pain tempered by his utter sense of humiliation at being stripped naked.

Umberto nearly gasped at the sight of the bronzed sleek demigod standing in the middle of the room; arms still yanked high above his head. A rich patch of arm pit hair now matted with sweat, a chest drenched in icy sweat, those perfect nipples elongated by the awkward position of his arms and shoulders, and then the sight of the long albeit narrow cock and the ball sack hanging down between his legs gave Umberto a sensation that he had never known before. Like a volcano rising from the depths, the blood began to flow in his veins. His excited heart beat like a wild drum tattoo, his cock grew rigid, and balls churned deep inside his guts. Alfredo looked over at the expression on his son's face and knew in an instant that he would be a worthy successor to rule, rule with blood and terror, the only way to keep the peasants and the other nobles in line.

Umberto's brow dripped a lustful sweat that stung his eyes. He took the back of his hand to rub away the sting yet never once averting his rapturous gaze from the strung up body before him.

"Please Count, please no more, I beg of you. I have a mother and two sisters that I have to support. Don't kill me or make it so I can't work. I am truly sorry about the horse. Please, no more."

But the young man's entreaties fell on deaf ears.

"Whip him, front and back, twenty strokes on each side and use the Roman flogger."

Davide had but to hear and he would obey. Taking the flogger with the iron tips from off the wall, the torturer give a few practice strokes to the air, then positioning himself behind his victim let forth a rain of blows. In three strokes, Francesco was screaming again, the sweat and blood forming a mist across his naked back and buttocks. His body fell forward in a vain attempt to escape the pain but to no avail. His shining chest, arched back, balls and cock thrust forward made of a sight of such beauty the Carlo could no longer contain him self. His cock throbbed wildly like a tethered animal till at last unable to contain itself shot forth in a spasm of unearthly bliss.

The punishing of Francesco was far from over as another twenty strokes of the flogger were applied to the man's chest leaving angry red welts crisscrossing his powerful torso and belly like licking flames; lacerating both his tits that dripped blood like tiny streams wending their way down his chest curving inward at his belly and ending in a single river dripping off the head of his cock. Several times the stable boy fainted only to be brought around by more water. It was well after midnight that the session ended. Francesco was cut down and left to crawl up the dungeon steps and into the night. Umberto and his father retired each to his on room, Umberto to reliving the last few hours and fondling himself into further ecstasy and Alfredo to drink himself into oblivion.

Yes, how vividly those memories played out on his feverish brain. Then thinking back to Carlo…

Ah, the first time, one always remembers the first time with such fondness Umberto sighed then with one fond final look of longing at the diabolical seat of torture and thoughts of Carlo swimming in his head he turned quickly from the dungeon and bounded up the blood spattered stone steps into the bright light of the castle's courtyard.

———————————

Carlo de Mazzini was the image of a Bellini bronze as the dappled sun light highlighted his copper colored hair and dark blood red cape, which billowed in the wind as he rode his magnificent Arabian mount towards Castle Orsini. He returned home after many long years of study though he had remained well informed about the unrest in and around the Orsini lands. Letters written by his father, his two brothers, and his father confessor filled him with deep foreboding. It would appear that the Old Count had turned into an insane tyrant, taxing his peasants to near starvation, torturing and executing anyone who stood in his way. Other letters told of his childhood friend, Umberto whose behavior seemed to mirror that of his diabolical sire. Carlo, out of desperation had even made an appeal to the Holy See but after waiting for weeks without an audience decided to take matters into his own hands. He would use as an excuse the failing health of his mother who in truth was languishing in bed from sadness over the suspicious death of her husband, Georgio de Mazzini.

———————————

The sun was casting's its final warm glow of the day over the Umbrian Hills as Carlo reached the outer gate of the family palazzo. He paused for a moment to enjoy the inviting sight of home, a place he had not seen for many years.

"What beauty" he thought to himself but then his eyes drifted up the hill to the Orsini castle perched like a vulture on the highest hill above the town. So many childhood memories flooded his mind turned rancid now with the knowledge of the great evil that now dwelled in that once magical and inviting castle. "What could have happened to Umberto to change him so," he said again to himself. Then with a heavy sigh, he spurred his horse on up the hill to his own family manse.

"Carlo, dear Carlo, home at last" cried his mother from the small balcony above the main entrance. Carlo waved cheerily as he dismounted, handed the reins of his horse to the old groom, and bounded up the front stairs as his mother flew down the stairs and into his waiting arms.

"Carlo, dear sweet boy, you are so grown, so handsome son. Step back a little and let me look at you, no not so far, come hug me again" and with these words the old woman broke down in tears. The death of her husband, the passing of time her own exhaustion proved too much for the poor soul to bare. She collapsed into a dead faint to be lifted up and carried to a chaise in the main sitting room. Maids were summoned with sprits and damp cloths. After several hours of ministering ointments, tears and a few spoons of grappa the old lady revived.

"Carlo, you must stay away, you must go back to Rome out of the reach of the Orsini's."

"I know it was Alfredo that had your father killed. Oh, it was said he died from falling off a horse but I saw his body as we prepared him for his final rest and those bruises and burn marks were not from a fall. No my dear, not at all," she said through her tears.

"Why would the Orsini's want to murder father?"

"Because he threatened to expose their evil to the Vatican. You have been gone a long time now; you have no idea of what horrors go on in the evil place. They are the devil's disciples, the father, and son. So many young men from the farms and village have vanished over the years or the bodies found trampled, mutilated, and left to rot in the forest or stream. The Orsini's say it is the work of highway men or accident but we all know this is not true. NO, you must not stay," the old lady shrieked her final words before falling into a troubled sleep.

Carlo placed a blanket over his mother, gave instructions for the chambermaids to keep an eye on her then retired to his room for some much-needed sleep.

"Luigi, have the stable boys saddle my horse," he instructed the major domo coming down the stairs.

"Yes Sir."

In less then a half hour Carlo was half way up the hill to Castle Orsini. Whispering cypress trees lined the steep and winding road to the drawbridge. This vestige of the dark ages was a powerful reminder of the power that resided behind those portals. How out of place Carlo thought, these vestiges of times long gone. Now at the height of the enlightened age these tyrants must be destroyed. How sad it was he thought that his once dear friend Umberto had succumbed to the old Latin maxim that "power destroys."

The drawbridge was already lowered by the time Carlo reached the final climb.

―――――――――――――――――――

"Welcome my dear friend Carlo," gushing with warmth said Umberto.

But Carlo could not help but notice that his old friend was flanked by two rather fearsome looking thugs; brandishing swords along with ill-concealed stilettos tucked in their boots.

154

"It has been a very long time Carlo."

"Yes Umberto, too long dear friend."

"And tell me how is his Holiness is doing, in good health I trust. We understand you spent some time at the Holy See and quite recently we hear."

"It is about that I have come to see you Umberto."

"Then by all means, enter please. My father is away in Mantua at the moment but we shall dine, just the two of us, like old times. My two friends here will take care of your horse."

With a wide grin, Umberto ushered Carlo into the castle's vast dinning hall where a lavish lunch was already laid. Strange, thought Carlo, how did he know I was coming?

"Take a seat, here let me pour you some wine."

"Thank you, Umberto."

"Why did you leave us Carlo?"

"You know why Umberto, I wanted to study law. I wanted to do something with my life, make a little difference in the world."

"I thought you loved me," Umberto whispered as he poured the blood red wine into the silver goblet, spilling just a drop as his hand shook ever so slightly.

"I did, but we were young then Umberto. Now please, let us talk of more urgent things."

These last few years, I have received letters, heard things about the Orsini family that frankly I was loathe to believe at first, things too terrible to even mention."

"What by thunder do you mean, be clear!"

"Disappearances, tortures, farms being confiscated by your family and given to your friends and…."

"And, and, get to the point."

"And the death of my father."

"Ah, that is it. That was an accident, everyone knows that."

"I saw my mother yesterday when I returned home. She saw his body before it was prepared for burial. She was horrified. Said his injuries were caused not by a simple fall from a horse. What do you know of this Umberto, for the sake of our friendship, what do you know about this?"

Umberto sat back in his chair and was silent for a moment, "Drink up Carlo, let us finish lunch, then I will tell you what I know, come drink."

Carlo reluctantly raised the goblet to his lips and took a few reluctant sips.

The remainder of the meal, which included a particularly salty boar roast, was consumed in silence. Carlo finished his wine and asked for more to slake his thirst. Umberto was happy to oblige. Carlo did not note that Umberto had not taken a sip from his goblet.

———————————————

"Carlo, wake up dear friend," Umberto cooed.

Carlo with aching head slowly opened his eyes but at first could not focus. He saw only shadows hovering about. It wasn't till a bucket of icy water cascaded over his head that he began to realize his predicament. First, the smell of rancid urine soaked hay filled his nostrils nearly making his wretch. He tried to move but found that his feet had been bound together with chain and padlocked. His wrists were tied together with a rope that was looped through an eyebolt embedded some five feet above in the stonewall causing distress in his shoulders.

As the clouds slowly drifted from his brain he saw standing by the cell door Umberto flanked by the two thugs he had seen earlier in the courtyard.

"Carlo, I hope you had a pleasant night's rest?"

"Umberto, what is this, I don't understand, what...." Carlo's words were cut short by Uumberto's instructions, "Strip him, and bring him to the chamber." Umberto turned quickly and strode down the passage to check on the preparations for Carolo's visit.

"You two listen to me, listen, my family has lots of money, hidden money, Umberto's is mad, let me go and my family will reward you, please you must listen, for your soul's sake if nothing else, please." Carlo begged as the two minions with practiced skill untied the lad, stood him up against the cold stonewall and began to strip him naked. The ugliest of the two, one Ottavio by name removed the stiletto from his boot top and began to deftly cut Carlo's shirt and under garment, leaving the shredded garment to fall in ribbons on the floor. Carlo tried to struggle but a sharp knee to his groin from the second henchmen, Flavio left him helpless, gasping for air, and trying to fight the urge to vomit. With lightning speed, his boots, socks, pantaloons, and undergarments were removed leaving the trembling man to stand naked and shivering from fear and the dungeons cold. Flavio and Ottavio stood back a little to admire the Adonis that they had so deftly stripped.

"Not a bad looking lad, eh Flavio?"

"Not bad at all, nice, pretty as a woman. And look at the balls on this one."

"He'll need 'em. Besides, the Master loves to work a man's nuts. Seen him mash 'em slow so the poor wretch lost his mind from the pain. Come on son, get a move on, don't want to keep Master Umberto waiting, now do we?"

Carlo tried to stand upright still hurting from the blow to his balls. He wanted to show these brutes what an aristocrat was made of so with every once of strength and fighting a near over-whelming fear he squared his shoulders, thrust out his chest, held his head high and despite the humiliation of his nakedness marched between his escort, out of the holding cell.

———————————————

The corridor was low, dank, and dark with only two smoldering torches placed in iron sconces to light the way. Carlo could not help but wonder how many other men had walked this way and if any had survived. He thought of his father who perhaps met his end in the very place. And what of his poor mother if he were to die here, alone and uncared for. No, he must not loose hope, perhaps Umberto would could to his senses, remember their childhood together, perhaps he could save Umberto from this demon that possessed his soul. With blood pounding in his ears, he marched along ready to face whatever God or man had in store.

———————————————

The massive stained oak door opened by an unseen hand. Carlo nearly gasped at the sight before him. There in the vaulted chamber stood Umberto, stripped to the waist, his massive hair-suit chest glistening in the light from the wall mounted torches and the coal brazier glowing on its tripod. Two pieces of furniture adorned the room. Sitting foursquare in the center of the chamber was the rack. A massive oaken relic from the dark ages, its well worn slats rubbed smooth from the countless sweating bleeding backs that had been pulled apart by its well worn ropes, ankle and wrist stocks and massive drum. But most alarming of all was the sight of the chair. Mounted on a stone pedestal the monster was fitted with eight iron hinges, like waiting arms to embrace a beloved.

Under the chair was an iron box open in the rear for the easy placing of coals.

"Carlo, come in, come in."

Flavio and Ottavio each grab one of Carlo's arms and lead him to stand a few inches from Umberto who nearly shook with excitement and lust for the sight before him.

Taking a deep sigh Umberto whispered, "Carlo my God you are so beautiful. Your hair is so lustrous, your skin like silk, those eyes, Carlo I could so easily loose my soul in the those eyes, and here" as he touched his nipples with his hands, "these rosebuds are so tantalizing." With the delicacy of a practiced courtesan, Umberto let his fingers glide over the two tits, brushing them gently, taking each nub between thumb and forefinger. Pressing down ever so lightly at first, staring like a cobra into Carlo's eyes all the time, he began to exert more and more pressure, adjusting his thumb nails to dig into the sensitive flesh. Deeper and deeper his nails pressed down but Carlo gave no sign of the slightest discomfort.

"Ah, I had forgotten you like to have your tits played with dear friend. That is good for they shall be given more then their share of pleasure this day."

"Umberto, why are you doing this? You say I am dear to you, that you find me desirable and yet you bring me here. Why, no matter what you are about to do to my body, you at least owe me an explanation."

"Carlo it is because I find you beautiful it is because I love you that I must make you suffer and destroy that very thing that I adore. Do you no understand dear friend?"

"Umberto, for your immortal soul, you can stop this now. You can free me; we will pray together, go to the Holy Father in Rome, and pray for forgiveness. Repent Umberto, become a worthy successor to the Orsini name."

"Carlo, it is too late. I am already damned beyond all redemption. Flavio, Ottavio, make our guest comfortable, let him rest awhile on the rack and so he doesn't fall and hurt himself, place his wrists and ankles in the stocks."

"Umberto, don't do this, for your sake."

"Hush friend, I wish now only to hear you plead from your eyes. Flavio, gag him."

Carlo, like a proud prince advanced to the rack. The two henchmen went about the work with well-rehearsed efficiency, having placed many a peasant and noble on this very instrument. Ottavio reached into his pocket and took an old rag he carried about and stuffed it into their captive's already dry mouth then secured it with a bit of rope he found lying on the floor.

First, the ankle stocks were opened as Carlo's feet were

placed in each of the half moons, then the top bar was placed and a loose bolt dropped into place, securing the victims' feet. The well-worn wooden holes had been stained from blood and sweat as other struggling men had their ankles rubbed raw from the pressure forced on their bodies by the giant drum.

Carlo offered little resistance as his arms were lifted over his head, placed in the wrist stocks, and were fastened in a similar manner. Eyebolts at each corner of the stock were threaded through with thick hempen rope that was loosely wound around a giant drum at the head of the rack. An improvised ship's wheel protruded from the side of the drum that was used for tightening and releasing of the ropes.

Umberto leaned against a far wall watching his men do their work. His heavy breathing, bulging eyes, and sweat-drenched brow were like signs of a randy lover. He could already feel the warmth form his heart spread to his groin as his manhood began to engorge with blood, stiffening his mighty rod.

"Flavio, turn the drum. I will tell you when to hold."

With an expression of cold indifference, Falvio proceeded to place his hands on the wheel and began to take up the slack. The drum turned slowly, creaking and rumbling in its mounting. The ropes together tightened; first lifting off the flat surface, engaging the wrist stocks to begin to pull the young man's arms ever tighter over his head. Carlo felt the first murmurs of discomfort in his wrists as the wooden holes chafed against his skin. A few more turns and Carlo felt the keen pull on his elbows and shoulders. The skin on his chest and abdomen tightened bringing in to high relief the perfect musculature of his fine athletic body. His ankles began to press painfully against the wooden cuffs sending small waves of pain into his shins and down into his feet. The pulling on his chest and abdominal muscles began to make it more and more difficult for Carlo to take deep breaths. He focused his gaze up into the darkness of the vaulted chamber trying with all his concentration to blot out the growing fear and pain that threatened to consume his resolve.

"Carlo, dear Carlo, you are so brave, so strong. If you only knew how alluring you look stretched out on the table," said Umberto as he placed his right hand on Carlo's chest. He could feel his beloved's strong heart beat.

"Yes, this is only the beginning. Here, let me untie the gag for a moment, I would like to hear your voice."

"Umberto before it is too late for you stop this. You may make me suffer for a few hours or even days but think of your immortal soul Umberto, think I beg of you. You will suffer for all eternity far worse then you could ever inflict on my body."

"Not what I wanted to hear Carlo" he replied as he once more stuffed the filthy rag into Carlo's resisting mouth.

"Favio, go to the shelf and bring me the long needles."

"Yes master" Flavio replied as he crossed the room.

"Here, give them to me. Yes, Carlo, let me show these two you. I have here three needles. See how long and sharp they are? What diabolical craftsmanship wrought their deadly beauty do you think? Ah, I forget you can't answer. Well let me explain. I had these made for us when last we were in Pisa. They have pierced the tender flesh of many of our enemies. Can you imagine where I will place them on you dear Carlo? Ah, foolish me, again, the gag prevents you from speaking. Very well, I will tell you. For you I shall place one through each of your tits then the third shall go down the length of that glorious cock of yours. Note if you will, how perfect and fine are their points but how they taper outwards. He let me try one for you. Which nipple should we begin with do you think?

Here, let us start with the left."

Carlo tried to steel himself for the piercing.

He tried not to look down to his chest as he felt Umberto grab and pull his right tit away from his body. The intensity of the pectoral muscle being yanked so far away from his rib cage and slight prick of the needles point as it position itself for entry made him cast his glance down his rib cage just as he felt the pricking turn into jabbing, piercing, burning invading agony. He clamped down on his jaw, sweat springing forth from his brow momentarily stinging and blinding his vision. He tried desperately not to scream but the wave of pain and the slowly advancing needle to the other side defeated his resolve. Through the muffling rag, he let forth a pitiful cry as he shook his head back and forth spraying perspiration across the room.

"Ah, you are enjoying that dear Carlo" Umberto remarked as he felt the tip of the needle pierce the other side of the skewered flesh.

"There now, that looks very good on you. Rest a moment Carlo; take some breaths while I admire my handiwork. Why I might have been a great maker of tapestries, such fine needle work."

Carlo's right tit was pierced through. The thickness of the needle could be discerned beneath his pectoral muscle like some horrible snake had burrowed beneath the young man's flesh. Only a slight trickle of blood wended its way down his taught rib cage forming tiny droplets on the wooden slats below.

"Well, you seem ready for the left side. Umberto leaned across Carlo, the weight of his body pressing against the pierced right tit sending yet more waves of chilling pain into already brutalized nipple. With much more speed then the first, Umberto quickly and deftly pierced the left nipple. The searing suddenness of the jab sent another nearly overpowering agony. Again, Carlo turned his head back and forth so violently that Umberto feared his victim-love would snap his neck.

"There now, perfect semitry" Umberto said as he pulled back to admire his handiwork.

"Yes you look very handsome now."

Carlo tried to speak through his gag but the buildup of saliva and the furious intake of breaths had lodged the rag even further down the young man's throat. Umberto, fearing the Carlo might suffocate removed the gag.

"There now Carlo, try to breath, take deep breathes. There are many more miles to go before you can rest."

"Please Umberto, please." Carlo managed to whisper.

"No Carlo, no. When you left me for Rome how many times did I beg you to return to me, saying please so many times my hand could write the word by its self, but did you return, no. You were too busy in your pointless pursuit of the law and fame to think of me and my loneliness. No Carlo, I have much more for you" Umberto replied as he slowly made his way to down along the length of the rack stopping near the man's groin.

Holding up the third and last needle with his right hand, Umberto grasped Carlo's dick in his left, pulled the rod up, and taught.

Carlo's eyes nearly leapt from their sockets as he both felt and saw what was about to happen to his manhood.

"Why?" Carlo screamed the one word out with all his strength as he felt the sharp prick of the needle being positioned at the lips of piss hole. His cry echoed off the vaulted ceiling, bounced from the stonewalls and floors but could not penetrate Umberto's heart.

Then a heinous soul crushing unbearable agony flooded Carlo's senses. His entire being seemed to center on the head and length of his cock as the needle progressed ever downward. Tears welled up in his eyes, sweat poured off his body pooling and further staining the rough wooden slats of the rack.

"Hold his head you two. No point in him knocking himself out" Umberto charged his two accomplices as Carlo tried desperately to raise his head and bang it down on the wooden planks. Flavio grabbed Carlo's full head of thick raven hair and held it down while Otavio placed his hands to either side of the young man's face preventing him from snapping his neck.

Carlo's body shivered as though he had seen the very pit of hell then with final gasp and scream he passed into blessed oblivion.

"He's fainted Master," Flavio observed.

"Yes idiot, I can see that. Let him rest awhile. Don't want his heart to give up yet. He needs some rest. While he's resting, fire up some coals then once he has revived will make him comfortable on the chair."

"As you lordship wishes," Ottavio said still showing little interest save that of the loyal functionary.

"I'll get the coals ready Ottavio" offered Flavio

Carlo's mother arose from her sick bed the following morning and straight away sent for her son.

"Signora, Carlo left for Castle Orsini yesterday morning. We have not seen nor heard anything since him then," said her housekeeper who was busy dusting a hallway bust.

"Good Lord in Heaven. Fetch Luigi right away, run!" she shouted to the old woman who managed to descend the stairs with some degree of haste calling out for Luigi, the major domo to the household.

"Yes Signora" he voice could be heard ascending the kitchen steps, "I am coming."

"Luigi, I fear for my son. He has not been heard from since yesterday. I am so afraid," she sobbed nearly swooning into old Luigi's frail arms.

"Signora, what can we do?"

"Find a stable boy to take a message. Get me paper and pen at once, at once," she shrieked as she made her way to her own dressing room.

Pen and paper appeared in good time for the distraught mother to pen her missive to the Holy Father in Rome begging him to send a Nuncio, an entire delegation if needs must straight away to investigate the goings on at Castle Orsini. Signora Begnalio had known Pope Manulus since he was boy and relayed on his previous kindnesses to her family as Bishop of Lucca to hear her cry for help.

"Now quick as lighting send this to Rome. Here take this ring with our family crest to give to the Holy Father as a token. Hurry for pity of all the saints. My son's life I know is grave danger. Go, Go."

"Yes Signora. The messenger is already saddled."

Luigi with old legs trembling nearly tumbled down the stairs, and out to the waiting horseman as the Signora Benaglio kneeled down in front of a small altar to the Virgin, and prayed with all her soul's might.

Umberto sat quietly in the chamber as coal was brought for the fire and Carlo was allowed blessed sleep.

Not an ounce of pity did the torturer feel for his victim. He could not help but wonder at this lack of feeling for one that he had so worshiped. Umberto had to admit to himself that the sight of suffering Carlo. The expression of agony and terror on his face, the straining muscle, and sinew of his magnificent body, the sweat that glistened of his silken olive skin highlighting every curve and valley like some Michelangelo statue drove him to levels of ecstasy that he had never known before. Yes, damn to hell though he might be he could not resist this urge perhaps sent from the devil himself, but devil be damned he would see this through to the end. But how quickly should this be done. He knew that Carlo could only stand so much abuse before he went mad or his heart burst from the excessive pain. Yes, he thought, let him rest on the rack over-night. He would have the needles removed, let him recover a little before the final onslaught in the iron chair.

Umberto stretched, yawned, put on his shirt, and left the chamber stopping at the staple to choose a stable lad for a night's companion. He was in far to excited a state to be able to sleep without the comfort and release of mouth around his cock bringing him to climax as he replayed the sights and sounds of the days sport with Carlo.

The morning dawned with a fierce torrent of rain and wind that lashed the castle's turrets, whipped the stately cypress trees along the drive into a frenzy, and sent gusts of chill air racing through the damp corridors and rooms. Umberto woke slowly, noticed the night's lad still tied spread eagled between the posts at the foot of the bed. The young's man head hung down on his chest but the slight rise and fall of his chest gave proof that the night's revelries had not done him in. His chest, back and legs were covered in angry red welts and lightly bleeding lacerations, hic cock and balls also showing signs of terrible abuse, tied up, and weighted, they hung black and blue between a pair of strong hairy legs.

Yes, thought Umberto, this fellow would live to see another day and perhaps once he recovered might be of some further use. But now it was time to return to Carlo.

He had his valet call Otavio and Flavio and commanded them to meet in the dungeon.

After washing, dressing, and the taking of a hearty breakfast of polenta and eggs, Master Umberto Orsini descended the well-worn steps into the dungeon.

Otavio and Flavio were already inside, replacing the spent coals in the fire, a bucket standing at the ready to carry them to the chair's box when they were called for.

Carlo still bound on the rack lay in a pool of sweat. His nipples and cock-swollen black and blue from the previous day's torture. His body shook more from a fever of infection then from fear. He had made his piece with God during the long black and lonely night of agony. He felt such despair at first but somehow he knew he would be rewarded in heaven when he would meet his family. But from out of his blissful reverie, the bang of the chamber door swinging open, the flurry of activity brought him back to unlooked for awareness.

"Carlo, you slept well I trust?"

Carlo cast his gaze across the room but exhaustion and fever prevented him from responding.

"Flavio, bring some water to revive our guest."

Without a word, the grey always obedient servant did as he was told. A pitcher of cold water was poured first over Carlo's head then with the remainder, it was drenched on his aching chest and groin. Carlo shook like a trembling leaf in a summer storm at the chill water against his fevered skin.

"Untie him and get him into the chair."

"No, no, please Umberto, no more, kill me now for pity sake, please, end this, perhaps if you release me from this nightmare the heavens will look more kindly on you" Carlo managed to whisper through his parched and cracked lips.

But Umberto just moved aside to give room for Flavio and Otavio to go about their gastly work.

Carlo's feet and wrists were taken out of the heavy wooden stocks, his shoulders ablaze as the blood rushed into the frozen muscle and sinews. Unable to sit up, the two thugs, with no small effort, lifted the naked man from off the table and carried him to the embrace of the iron chair. Dropping their heavy burden down on the pyramid-encrusted seat brought forth a new avalanche of agony. The apex of hundreds of iron points dug into Carlo's back, ass, thighs, and fore arms. Only his swollen balls and cock rested lightly on the iron.

"Fasten the bars to his body and make them tight then bring me a weight to mash his manhood down" Umberto spoke in a monotone that masked his growing excitement at the unholy torments that were soon to come.

Carlo tired desperately to take a deep breath but he was only able to achieve small gasps for air as the pain was almost overwhelming his senses.

"Carlo, you must know that it is your fault and yours alone that you sit here now. Had you loved me, had you stayed with me to help me blot out these demons that posses my soul, you would be my constant life companion but now, now your life will soon end, and though I shall go on breathing and bringing more men here to my dungeon, it shall be as though I died with you. Bring the coals, fill the box."

Otavio and Flavio stoked the embers then with a coal shovel carried the burning nuggets across the chamber and placed them in the iron box. When at last the box was full to overflowing and slide into place Umberto placed a large stone between Carlo's legs mashing his manhood down into the points of the pyramids. The young man groaned softly at first but began to sob pitifully as Umberto increased the pressure impaling the scrotum but this sensation was nothing compared to the radiating heat that began to sear into Carlo's ass, thighs, and back. He started to scream, a scream that became a wail like an Irish banshee call. It grew and grew louder and higher and to such a fevered pitch, that it would have melted all of the world's ice.

Umberto stood back then and watched that horrible contortions and listened to the ear splitting cries unaware of the loud banging and yelling of the Swiss Guard. In but an instant the great oaken door swung open, six guards with halberds rushed into the room followed by the Nuncio himself.

"HOLD, HOLD THIS ABOMINATION" he commanded with all the power of the Holy Mother Church.

Umberto turned like a cornered tiger and leapt at the Nuncio, ready to strangle the cleric but the landing of a halberd on the back of his neck brought the attack to a sudden and deadly end.

"Remove him at once" the Nuncio ordered," and take these two sinners away to away judgment. Bring the young man above and remove him at once to his mother's care."

Carlo lay in agony for many days, unable to lie on his back or piss without screaming he finally recovered though he never spoke a word again but was lost in a fog of forgetfulness. When at last his mother died, a group of Franciscans took in Carlo where he spent his days in prayer.

About the Author

Will grew up on the Jersey shore where every summer was spent mostly on the beech reading, swimming and fantasizing about the hot men at the gay beach in Belmar.

He works in the theatre and writes for his own amusement taking as inspiration the work of Cavello, C. S. White, and of course *Greasetank* along with all the countless movies watched on Saturday afternoons with suffering bare chested heroes. William is interested in the psychology behind the torment of his imaginary victims and likes historic and exotic settings. He currently lives in New York.

www.ingramcontent.com/pod-product-compliance
Lightning Source LLC
Chambersburg PA
CBHW071219260626
47162CB00004B/1352